WAITING TO DISAPPEAR

April Young Fritz

HYPERION
BOOKS
FOR
CHILDREN
NEW YORK

ACKNOWLEDGMENTS

Special thanks to my agent, Steven Malk, for believing in my work, and to my editor, Andrea Davis Pinkney, for giving this book a home and helping to make it shine. And to all the people at Hyperion who helped to turn my manuscript into a finished work, especially David Cashion for his encouragement, I am deeply grateful.

To a special group of writers, Chapter Seven, thanks for the sisterhood and the support

Text copyright © 2002 by April Young Fritz

Printed in the United States of America

First Edition

3 5 7 9 10 8 6 4 2

The text for this book is set in 13-point Bembo.

Library of Congress Cataloging-in-Publication data on file.

ISBN 0-7868-0790-3 (tr.)

Visit www.hyperionchildrensbooks.com

For my children,
Michael, Megan, and Chelsea—
you fill my life with joy.

In memory of my grandmother
Fannie Martin Kelly,
my safe harbor

and of my uncle
William J. Kelly,
my hero

CHAPTER ONE

*A*UNT SHERRY came to stay the summer Mama left us. To hear my daddy tell the tale, you'd think Mama went away that hot July third. Facts don't recount the whole story. I carry the truth in my heart: Mama's spirit had flown away two years before on the day my brother Booth died, May 10, 1958.

She needs time, Daddy reminded me whenever I asked him when we'd get Mama back, the real Mama who smiled with her whole face and not just her lips. After two years, I grew impatient.

The summer of Mama's "episode," as Daddy

referred to her breakdown, started out with temperatures so cool, most mornings I pulled on the chenille robe hanging from my bedpost. Just when I thought I'd never see the sun again, a heat wave moved into Moodus and lingered, an unwelcome guest who forgot to go home. Each time I stepped outside, I swallowed air so hot and moist it about cooked the inside of my mouth. The humidity wreaked havoc on our Emerson Quiet Cool; it seized up more times than I could count. I took to sleeping in a canvas tent on the porch with my dog, Pepper, a pointer Mama and I had rescued from the pound where we volunteered. Most nights I wore cotton shorty pajamas and lay in the tent reading mysteries and old copies of *Silver Screen* magazine by flashlight, a bag of cherry licorice whips at my side.

Mama spent the week with her ear tuned to WKLM listening to the weather reports. She fretted it might rain and the neighborhood picnic would need to move from our back field to inside our house; the thought of forty-odd people crammed within its walls with its temperamental plumbing and one bathroom caused her to twitch every time the sky darkened.

The morning of the episode, Mama went into town to shop for the picnic. Pepper was off chasing squirrels and I was sitting on the porch, cooling myself with a paper fan made from the Sunday comics, when a red Impala convertible, my Aunt Sherry at the wheel, zipped along our driveway, spreading clouds of dust in its wake.

The Impala came to a screeching halt under the red maple, its tires spewing stray pieces of gravel. The driver's door popped open, and I watched Sherry jump from her perch, a streak of black in her sleeveless knit top and capri pants. She stood almost six feet tall, and the skintight pants ended high above her pink canvas espadrilles, their grosgrain ribbons laced around her calves, sinewy from years of ballet classes with Miss Lenore.

Sherry planted her feet on the driveway and shook herself loose, the way Pepper does after he swims in the pond. Her shaggy copper-colored hair cut the air like so many knives. *Pfft, pfft, pfft.* She had hacked off her waist-length hair with a pair of kitchen shears late one night, after her high-school sweetheart called from college to inform her he was dumping her for someone he had met in his American history class.

I still hadn't gotten used to her new look. As she opened the rear door to the car, a cluster of wire-thin silver bracelets chimed against her wrists. I spotted Gram sitting hunched in the backseat, waiting for someone to announce that it was okay to move. She wore a plastic rain bonnet to keep her hair in place.

I remained on the porch, still as a sentry, content to observe my aunt perform her tasks unaware of my presence. Still and waiting is how I spent that summer. Waiting to turn fourteen, waiting for something to happen. I became ever watchful, the town crier of the small world that was my family.

Pepper chose that moment to return from his hunt through the back fields. Bounding around the side of the house, he stopped dead in his tracks to bark a warning.

Sherry told him to hush up, turned to me, and smiled. "Buddy, come help," she called. I ran across the drive, my legs shaky with anticipation. For me, Aunt Sherry was Sandra Dee and Miss America rolled into one. She had turned twenty-two that June and sold cosmetics at the JCPenney over in Sandy Springs. I admired her ability to change her look quicker than a chameleon; she wore a different color lipstick with matching nail polish every day of the week.

Compared to Sherry, I felt as plain as a brown-paper bag. A growth spurt in the eighth grade shot me from five feet two to five-six, most of it in my legs. My weight lagged behind, leaving me with the look of a yearling in need of sweet feed.

Mama used to try to do something with my hair. The year I turned ten, after one too many Tonette home permanents with their stinky lotion and tor-ture rods, I put my foot down and told Mama my straight, brown, flyaway hair was just fine with me. Except for special occasions when I let Sherry smear it with Dippity-Do and roll it up on wire rollers, I fixed my hair in braids or a ponytail.

There was no one quite like my aunt Sherry. She told me some days she went to work wearing no underwear. Sherry had adventures. Once she drove clear to Virginia Beach with nothing but the clothes on her back, a makeup bag and a twenty-dollar bill. I figured if I stayed close to her, one day she'd take me along. My given name is Elizabeth, but Sherry gave me my nickname, Buddy, because I had been nipping at her heels since I took my first step. I would have followed Sherry into a burning building.

Back in the car, Gram cleared her throat loud enough to reach the cheap seats in the balcony. She watched me from where she sat in the middle of the backseat, piles of her handmade quilts layered into rippled stacks framing her like soft bookends, their bold colors a counterpoint to her paleness. I could tell by the set of her thin lips she wanted out of that Impala.

"I'm about to die from the heat," she announced, and stabbed a loose strand of gray hair with a bobby pin. "We would have been here earlier, but Sherry likes to sleep in. I told her last night we needed to get an early start, but nobody ever listens to me anymore."

"Maybe that's because you never stop complaining,

Hazel." Sherry had taken to calling Gram "Hazel" in the third grade because she looked so much older than everyone else's mama did. Gram had had Sherry two months shy of her forty-sixth birthday.

The two of them lived just on the other end of Moodus, in a hundred-year-old row house off Main Street, but to hear Gram tell it you would have thought they had come from California in a covered wagon. With Gram in harness. She didn't trust anyone's driving at night, so she planned to sleep over.

Sherry stood off to the side of the car out of Gram's view and rolled her eyes at me. I took hold of one of Gram's hands, the skin translucent and delicate as the tissue Mama wrapped around the glass Christmas ornaments, and eased her from the car. She sighed with relief as her small feet hit solid ground. With a quick motion, she pulled me to her, bending my neck like a gooseneck lamp and crushing my face against her soft chest.

"How's my girl? You been good?"

"Good as gold." I inhaled the scent left by a hot iron on her faded peach housedress and detected a hint of Evening in Paris from the blue glass bottle

7

she kept on her maple dresser. As I lifted my head I noticed how pink her scalp was, almost like a baby's. Fifty-four years apart in age, we were passing each other like elevators; me on my way up and Gram on her way down. I feared the day she'd be gone.

There was no sense to worry her with my premonitions, my sense of impending doom. Mama's "spells" wore her down real bad. Once, Mama and Sherry and their sister, Tess, fought about who would cook the turkey for Thanksgiving dinner, and Mama got so riled up that she hyperventilated and had to breathe into a brown-paper sack. Gram confided in me she prayed every day for her girls to get along. She said she awaited a sign someone was listening.

Sherry nudged me with her elbow and pushed her white plastic heart-shaped sunglasses to the top of her head. "So, Buddy, how's your summer going? Got a boyfriend?"

She leaned down and wrapped her arm around me. I loved how she did that. The way she looked like a movie star, all tall and shiny and inaccessible, and then in one swift motion came down to my size and made me feel important. As if I mattered.

"Ignore her, missy, she's got boys on the brain." Gram trudged across the sunburned grass, the twine strap of a Macy's shopping bag held tight in her hand. Gram traveled with her favorite cooking utensils the way some people travel with their best jewelry. She dropped the bag at her feet and collapsed on the glider set on the porch under the living-room window. "Bring me some ice water, will you, Buddy? I'm parched."

I fetched a red plastic tumbler of ice water for Gram and two bottles of Coke for Sherry and me. "Can I help?" I asked, as Sherry lugged Gram's scuffed blue Samsonite up the steps and deposited it near the door.

"No thanks, the rest can wait. One of those for me?" She pointed to the bottles on the windowsill.

"Sure. I figured you must be thirsty." I handed a Coke to her, its sides frosted just like the one on the poster in the drugstore. She popped the cap with the bottle opener hanging from a nail on the post.

"This tastes good." Sherry downed half the bottle and belched. "Where is everybody?"

"Mama's shopping for the picnic stuff and

Daddy's at the drugstore. He said he'd try to come home early if Darlene decides to show up and work the counter. I volunteered, but he said helping Mama was more important than mixing root-beer floats. Where's Aunt Tess?"

"She'll be along tomorrow morning. As usual, she put herself in charge of decorating the floats at the firehouse so she'll be busy until midnight."

My aunt Tess was the middle child, born five years after Mama and fifteen years before Sherry. Not quite the middle according to my calculations, but definitely centered in the eye of the storm. Tess favored Grandpa's side of the family, all shoulders and thighs, like one of those roller-derby women who shove each other around the ring on TV. Tess couldn't tell me the best shade of lipstick to wear or make me laugh like Sherry, but she was morally solid, and I could count on her to pull Mama back from the edge.

Tess taught phys ed at the high school, coached the girls' field hockey in the fall and the girls' track team in the spring. Mama was one of the two high-school guidance counselors, so she and Tess had lunch together every day in Mama's office with

;n on the door that said
.he thought of entering
ıall filled me with mixed emo-
ma and Tess, I didn't stand a
' with anything.

ater and set the glass on the
Ier swollen puffball ankles
dges of her white leather
'eather ones in the winter,
nclement weather. Gram
believed clothes should be practical.

"I need to lie down for a few minutes." She
pointed to her suitcase. "Put that in my room, will
you, Sherry? I'm going to get a bite to eat from the
kitchen to tide me over until dinner."

"I'll get you something, Gram," I said. "You can
rest here on the glider." I needed to keep her out of
the house until Mama got home.

The calm exterior with its swept porch and pots
filled with red geraniums concealed the chaos
inside. Gram would scold me for not tidying up the
place. How could I make her understand I did the
best I could?

Mama was the queen of clutter and forbade me to move so much as a piece of paper without her permission. She held on to the past the only way she knew how; my brother Booth's varsity jacket still hung from the peg next to the back door. I noticed her touch it every time she left the house, a talisman to keep us safe.

Gram waved me away. "You and Sherry do your girl talk. I need to use the facilities."

"Come sit a spell, Buddy." Sherry tilted her head.

I waited until the screen door had slapped shut behind Gram, then sat next to Sherry on the glider. I drank my Coke down until it was the same level as Sherry's, and then we played the game where we let the sweet liquid slip down our throat one drop at a time, seeing who could make hers last the longest.

I was winning when the door banged open, and Gram burst outside, a bruised banana in her hand. "What is going on, Buddy?" She waved the banana at me.

I sat up straight and faced her. Sherry remained still, her eyes closed.

"I'm talking about the house." She jabbed the banana in the direction of the doorway. "It looks like a tornado tore through the place and nobody noticed. Newspapers and laundry scattered hither and yon and there's not a scrap to eat in the kitchen. Not anything I would dare to put in my mouth. How does Ellen expect to feed all those people at the picnic tomorrow?"

"I told you, Mama's gone to Winn-Dixie. She's got her list."

"She'll need a miracle to fix all the food and get the house ready for company in less than"—Gram paused to look at her pink-gold watch, its expandable band pinching her fleshy wrist—"in less than twenty hours. Dear Lord, we're going to be up half the night slicing and dicing." Gram bit her lip and sighed. "Buddy, how's your mama been doing lately? You're not keeping anything from me, are you?"

"You worry too much, Hazel," said Sherry. She reached into her tote bag and pulled out a pack of Dunhills, the red-and-gold box a miniature jewel case.

Gram removed a hankie tucked beneath the belt

of her dress and used it to pat the perspiration from her face. "Spoken like the baby of the family. When was the last time you worried about anything except your hair and makeup?"

Sherry lit a cigarette, dropping the match into the pot of begonias. "Oh, boy, here we go."

Gram stood over me, her hand resting on my shoulder. "Buddy, you've been home all day. Why don't you help out your mama more?"

"I cleaned up the bathroom and scoured the kitchen sink, but Mama told me to hold off doing the other stuff until she got home. She likes to supervise."

"Well, if she's not careful, the lot of you will end up like those crazy Collyer brothers. The newspaper said they were found dead in their apartment, hidden by stacks of papers and magazines high as corn in August."

"Mama's not crazy!" The words came out louder than I intended, as if saying them at the top of my voice would make them true.

CHAPTER TWO

*D*ADDY CAME home at half past six, still wearing his white pharmacist's coat. It seemed like everyone in town decided they couldn't live without a bottle of aspirin or a tube of toothpaste two minutes before closing time. Darlene left him high and dry at five o'clock, saying she had to get to her hair appointment.

If I had known, I would have ridden my bike into town and waited on the customers myself. I'm real good at putting on a happy face and asking after their mamas, nodding my head in sympathy when they drown their sorrows in a coffee ice-cream soda and confide their troubles between sips and slurps. It's easy to keep track of who's under the weather when you're privy to the prescriptions of everyone in town. That's how I knew that someone in the Webster family had head lice and that Billy Roberts had got another ear infection.

Every time Daddy caught me reading a label on a prescription he warned me what I saw behind the counter was nobody's business. He had nothing to worry about; I have a talent for keeping secrets the way some people can hit high C. It just comes naturally.

Gram and I sat at the kitchen table with Sherry, who was painting her nails with Cherries in the Snow nail polish. We watched as Daddy, his shoulders slumped, stopped near the stove and worked his nose like a crazed rabbit, sniffing dead air.

"I don't smell any dinner," he announced.

"That's because there is none," said Gram. "We're all going to starve." She nudged me in the ribs and smiled. Gram loved to tease Daddy. She once told me he was a humorless man, a good provider, but not much fun.

"Where's your mama?" He rummaged in the refrigerator and came away with a pitcher of orange juice and a hunk of cheese he had found hidden behind a bowl of beans growing fuzz. I noticed Daddy had gotten a haircut; wide paths around Daddy's ears looked like they were made by a golf-course lawn mower.

"Mama's shopping for the picnic." I wondered myself what was taking her so long, but I needed to pretend there was nothing strange about her forgetting to come home.

"She left hours ago." Daddy pointed to the stove as if he were more concerned there was no dinner than that Mama'd gone missing.

"But, Daddy, she had a ton of places to go."

He had no idea what Mama did all day. Daddy's world was small; home and the drugstore comprised his universe. It's not that he didn't care, he loved Mama more than life itself, but his needs were simple; he failed to understand that not everyone was content to eat the same pot-roast-mashed-potato-and-peas menu for Sunday dinner for twenty-five years. After more than two decades of living with

Mama, he still hadn't noticed she was not June Cleaver, a woman who dusted every nook and cranny of her television house while wearing a pretty dress and high heels.

Mama's Saturday shopping routine never varied. First she went to the cleaners, then the library, Pick 'n Save, and finally Winn-Dixie. She saved the market for last so the frozen food wouldn't defrost before she could file it in the 16-cubic-foot Sears freezer taking up half the space in the mud room. She had bought it with her own money, explaining to Daddy how, in the long run, it would pay for itself. Personally, I believe she loved the idea of buying a major appliance without consulting him.

Most Saturdays she usually came clomping up the steps, her arms filled with heavy brown-paper sacks, long before dinnertime. After we had put away the groceries, she'd move her piles of junk from one end of the counter to the other to make a small space to prepare dinner. After dinner, she moved the stuff back, vowing to sort through the catalogues, clippings, and mail in the morning.

Please come home, Mama, I thought to myself as

I watched Daddy part the muslin curtains to peer outside, freeing the dust motes trapped in the ruffles.

"It's half past six, where could she be?" He retracted his head from between the curtains, turned, and studied the kitchen with the curiosity of someone thinking of buying the place. "Looks like you were busy cleaning today, Buddy. Your mama will be pleased."

That showed how much he knew about Mama. Try as I might, there was no way I could stop Gram from doing a long overdue spring cleaning, but Mama would blame me just the same.

"Gram cleaned the kitchen. And Sherry vacuumed the living room and the front hall. I scrubbed the bathroom and swept the porch."

Daddy nodded his head, then went back to keeping watch at the window. Gram took me aside and suggested I call and ask Mr. Beetles, the manager of the Pick 'n Save, if he had seen Ellen Mullens. The phone rang before I had a chance to dial.

"This is Mr. Tweedy, down at the Music Hall." It was Harvey Tweedy, a self-important man who had begun his career at the Music Hall as an usher during the era of stage shows and silent movies. He stayed on when it changed hands and CinemaScope came to Moodus. The new ushers couldn't care less if you broke your neck finding a seat in the dark, but he made them wear those moth-eaten maroon wool jackets with the frayed gold braid he had sported in his glory days.

"I need to speak with your daddy," he insisted. His voice squeaked the way it did when he hassled the kids to get their feet off the backs of the seats. "It's important."

"My daddy's not here." If he wanted to get me in trouble for sneaking into the theater the week before, why should I make it easy for him?

Daddy returned to the kitchen and asked me if it was Mama on the phone. I covered the mouth-piece and whispered, "It's for me."

He went upstairs to change his clothes. Sherry, who never could bear to miss out on anything, mashed her ear next to mine. We must have looked as if we were joined at the head.

"Are you still there, Buddy? It's about your mama, she's not feeling too well."

Visions of Mama clutching her chest caused my own heart to seize momentarily and then lurch against my ribs. "What's wrong with her?"

Gram sat up straighter than a soldier in the Queen's Guard. "What's going on?" she asked. I shushed her with a wave of my free hand.

Mr. Tweedy's voice buzzed through the receiver. "Now, don't be alarmed, Buddy, but it seems your mother was overcome by the movie or something because Junior Nevins found her crying in her seat when he was cleaning the popcorn off the floor. She kept muttering 'I'm sorry, I'm sorry,' and well, she took hold of Junior's hand and wouldn't let go."

The image of my mother holding hands with Junior Nevins scared me. Standing as tall and scraggly as an Irish wolfhound, his flashlight attached to his belt with a brass chain, he was a Mr. Tweedy in the making.

"Where is she now?" I closed my eyes and made a wish that when I opened them, Mama would walk through the door.

It was all a mistake, she would assure me. I opened my eyes. No Mama.

Gram stood and removed a terry dish towel from her Macy's bag and plucked at the loops. "Is this about Ellen?"

"Hush, Gram, I can't hear what he's saying."

Mr. Tweedy rattled on. "We got her as far as the refreshment stand and then Wanda took over, but we've got a problem on our hands, Buddy. Your mama is sitting still as a stone on a case of Milk Duds."

Sherry turned to Gram. "Ellen's not talking."

After a pause on the line, I heard Mr. Tweedy tell Wanda to get busy making the popcorn before the rush for the seven o'clock show.

"Does she want us to come get her?" I asked. Daddy came into the kitchen wearing a pair of patched khakis and a blue cotton shirt buttoned up to his neck. The stiff collar rumpled his soft chin.

"I don't know what she wants." Mr. Tweedy spoke in hushed tones. "One minute she is bawling her eyes out and then she settles down. Wanda thought I'd better call you."

"We'll be right down." I hung up the phone. Prickles of heat moved across my face and chest, but when I touched my skin as Mama did to detect a fever, it felt as cool and damp as the inside of an ice chest.

"Down where?" asked Gram.

"To get Mama. She's at the Music Hall."

"Was that your mama on the phone?" Daddy stood near the kitchen door, his brow furrowed into deep rows. "Buddy, who was on the phone?"

Gram headed for the door in her scuffed blue leather house shoes, still wearing her bib apron.

"Is anyone going to tell me what's going on?"

Sherry pulled Daddy aside and broke the bad news in her own tactful way. "Ellen's gone nuts or something. Mr. Tweedy said she was holding hands with Junior Nevins down at the Music Hall and now she's sitting on a case of Milk Duds. As far as I'm concerned it's about time. She's been holding everything in for too long. Trying to be a saint can kill a person."

I tried to imagine Mama with her arms wrapped around herself real tight, holding in her troubles, but I couldn't bring her into focus. Mama didn't hold everything in so much as lock everyone out; I couldn't remember the last time she had let me into her heart.

Someone had to do something; we couldn't leave her there. Gram stood at the door, her hand rattling the knob.

"One of us better go fetch her." Sherry reached for her bag on the kitchen counter. "We need to leave. Now."

She herded Daddy and me toward the door, using her long arms to corral us. I wanted to show her I was not some wishy-washy kid who went to pieces as soon as a crisis came to visit, but when I removed the car keys from the blue china bowl on the counter, my fingers turned to wood and the keys slipped to the floor.

Daddy stooped to retrieve them. "It's all right, Buddy," he whispered to me. "Everything will be all right."

He led me to the Buick, where Gram waited in the backseat, the lines of her face sunk deep with worry. Sherry sat next to her, a look of anticipation on her face like the one she'd had the time we headed off to bring Pop Pop home from the Dew

Drop Inn, where he had done a little too much celebrating after winning the euchre tournament. Sherry thrived on turmoil.

Daddy drove and I filled him in on Mr. Tweedy's message. "She was fine when I left this morning," he said. I knew he must be scared because he ran a red light, and Daddy prided himself on his unblemished driving record.

I wanted to scream at him, *Are you blind? Didn't you see how she looked?* but the words wedged in my throat when I noticed how his hands trembled as he gripped the steering wheel.

Mama had seemed preoccupied that morning, wandering in and out of rooms looking like someone who forgot what she had come for. She mumbled off things from her to-do list, her eyes darting in a thousand directions. She left the house without combing her hair; its frizzy brown curls puffed around her face like a cloud left after an explosion. Dressed in her faded denim jumper from the Trade-A-Way, she wore penny loafers run down at the heels and white anklets that didn't match; one sock stood an inch higher than the other; lipstick smudges framed her mouth.

How could Daddy not have noticed? When did my parents stop looking at each other? I was no better. I sensed her sadness becoming heavier, pulling her down. But I did nothing about it except ask her if she needed help with dinner or make her a cup of tea when she got home from spending all day listening to teenagers complain about how much they hated school. We talked, but we didn't say anything. We played hot potato with our sadness.

Daddy claimed Mama worked too hard, spread herself too thin volunteering her time to anyone who asked and rescuing every stray animal that came along. He needed to believe her when she told him she was never better; Daddy didn't see anything that would stir up the pot.

The day my brother Booth died, Mama ceased being Mama. Like a picture left too long in the sun, she faded away until all I could see was an outline. Her silly laugh was gone; she could barely manage a smile.

Gram tells me I am the barometer of the family. I'm able to sense change before it happens the way she can feel rain in her arthritic knees. This gift is both a blessing and a curse. What good is it to be able to look into someone's soul and see their pain if you can't fix it? I knew what caused Mama's sadness; I also knew nothing I could do would make it go away. She was disappearing from the inside out like a thousand-year-old egg. One day there would be nothing left of her but a shell.

I needed to do something, but I felt weak and afraid to face her. The closer we got to the Music Hall, the more I wished Daddy would leave me by the side of the road.

"You're going to get us killed," yelled Gram from the backseat, still clutching the kitchen towel. "Ellen isn't going anywhere, so slow down."

"Worrywart," said Sherry under her breath.

We left the car parked in the fire lane in front of the Music Hall on Main Street. Daddy and I sprinted across the pavement until we skidded to a stop at the inner doors of the theater.

Mr. Tweedy looked relieved to see us. "Not a minute too soon," he said.

Gram and Sherry caught up to us and pushed past Mr. Tweedy. He flailed his hands and shouted after us, "I'd like to help you, but I can't leave my post."

"The man is an idiot," said Gram. As we approached the refreshment stand, she took my hand and gave it a reassuring squeeze. Sherry lingered near the movie posters on the wall, the lookout man.

The burnt-butter smell of popcorn hung in the air. I peered over the refreshment counter to see Wanda Hemmings perched on the large cardboard carton next to Mama, its side crushed under her weight. She reminded me of my nursery-school teacher, Miss Post, the way she talked to Mama real soft and stroked her hair back from her face.

"Ellen, your family is here. Look, even your mama's come to take you home." Wanda turned Mama's face in our direction.

Mama stared up at us as if she couldn't quite place where she'd seen us before. Recognition came into her eyes and she burst into tears. I was not born without a brain; common sense told me to rush to her side and hug her to me. My feet would not budge.

I was thanking the powers that be that no one I knew from school was there when my luck ran out and Teresa Potter from my Home Economics class came strolling in with her gang of juvenile deviants from the Moodus Pep Squad. Fortunately, they headed straight for the restroom to apply a third coat of makeup.

"Come on, let's go home. You'll feel better after you've had a cup of tea." I gave Mama's sleeve a tug. She recoiled like a frightened caterpillar.

"We have to go now, Ellen. It's almost time for your favorite shows." Daddy jangled the coins in his pocket.

Gram told him to hush; she knelt in front of Mama. "Look at me, Ellen. Whatever is bothering you, we can talk about it at home."

Mama stared at the floor, a low humming sound escaping her pinched lips, like a lightbulb about to burn out.

"Get up, Mama," I demanded. "Why is she doing this?" I wanted to die or kill someone. Daddy answered me with a sigh of exasperation. His cheeks flushed red.

I looked around the lobby and noticed the paths worn into the floral carpet. If only I could follow one of those paths out of the theater, wander the streets of Moodus until some nice family took me in and called me their own. A normal family with parents who didn't do anything to call attention to themselves.

Gram tugged on my hand. "I wish Tess were here. She'd know what to do. Buddy, go call her." I pulled away and leaned against the popcorn machine.

Sherry's ears perked up at the mention of Tess; she left her post to join us. "Well, hell's bells, Tess is sitting on her fat ass in a firehouse playing with chicken wire and crepe paper so she can have the best float in the parade third year in a row. If you ask my opinion, Ellen is not going to move of her own accord. I say it's up to us to get her out of here before a photographer for *The Moodus News* gets wind of this and we all end up on the front page."

Sherry took our silence as consent and mobilized the four of us into a human transport system. Each of us took one of Mama's limbs and carried her through the Music Hall foyer and out to the car. I prayed for the Lord to take me at the first sight of anyone I knew.

CHAPTER THREE

WE DEPOSITED Mama on the backseat of the Buick; she ignored us as if she were a passenger in a taxi waiting for us to start the meter. I sat next to Daddy in front, biting my lip until it hurt.

I closed my eyes and an image of Mama appeared beneath my eyelids. She circled above me, spinning into space as I struggled to reach her, desperate as a child stretching to recapture a kite blown free from her grasp.

Daddy put the car in gear and we drove around to the back of the theater. There sat Mama's wagon parked all herky-jerky, the wayback crowded with brown-paper sacks from Winn-Dixie.

Daddy rummaged through Mama's purse to find the keys. He handed them to Sherry. "Follow us home," he said.

We drove home, Gram staring at the bald spot on the back of Daddy's head and patting Mama's hand until I thought she would turn it into hamburger. Mama made ticking sounds with her tongue.

Sherry followed close behind us in Mama's car; she had the radio on loud enough for me to hear the music.

A sky shimmering with the first evening stars sheltered our darkened house. Daddy pulled the car into the driveway. "We're home, Ellen," he said.

Mama's body began to shake. The cords stood out on her neck. She pushed away Gram's hand and bent over as if she were preparing for a crash landing.

Daddy let out a puff of air, jerked himself from the car, and motioned for the rest of us to join him. Gram hobbled from the car. "We can't leave her there."

"What do you want me to do?" Daddy did not

deal well with upset; he once told me he loved pharmacology because it was a precise science.

Sherry walked over and offered Mama a cigarette. When that got no response, Sherry left two cigarettes, and a book of matches, "Just in case."

"Mama? Are you okay?" I leaned into the car, careful not to touch her.

"Go away, Buddy." She didn't say it in a mean way, but in a soft, pleading voice.

"Let's leave her alone for a few minutes. She'll come in when she's ready." Sherry tapped my arm and pulled me away from the car. Even Gram urged me to let her be for a spell.

Mama fooled all of us, because in one quick motion, she yanked the car keys from Daddy's hand, locked the doors and turned the Buick into a fortress.

"For heaven's sake, Ellen. What do you think you're doing?" Daddy pulled at the door handle.

She turned away from him, covering her ears. Gram pressed her face to the window. "This is not like you, Ellen. Why don't you come inside and have a cup of tea. You don't have to talk."

"Let me be," Mama said. She looked at me, then covered her face with her hands. "And take Gram with you."

Gram looked pathetic standing there in her faded apron, her face pinched with worry. "Okay," I said, and patted the window like a visitor saying good-bye to a prisoner trapped behind glass. It didn't feel right leaving her alone, but what else could I do?

Sherry stayed outside on the front porch where she could smoke and keep an eye on Mama. Daddy rummaged in the refrigerator, sniffing packages of olive loaf and liverwurst as he removed them from the meat bin. Pepper circled us like a hungry shark. I gave him a piece of cheese, and he rewarded me with sloppy kisses before pestering Daddy for some of his food.

Daddy tossed him a slice of olive loaf, then loaded hunks of liverwurst between two pieces of stale bread and slathered his creation with brown mustard.

"Do you want something, Buddy? Gram?"

"How can you expect me to eat when my daughter is having a nervous breakdown in the front yard?" Gram insisted on making me a peanut-butter sandwich.

I managed to eat a few bites, more to please her than to satisfy a hunger. Daddy could eat no matter what. He was practically the only one who had eaten at Booth's wake, and in the past two years, he'd put on forty pounds.

I heated water for tea. Sherry came inside just as the whistle blew. She proceeded to take over, brewing tea in the English cottage teapot, laying out china, sugar and cream, and a plate of graham crackers on the pine table near the window. After pouring for us, she helped herself to a beer. Gram and I sipped our tea, and Sherry continued her vigil over Mama from the kitchen window.

At ten o'clock Daddy gave up and went to bed. "She'll come in when she's ready."

"We can't leave her out there." The skin on Gram's face sagged, pulling her mouth down at the corners; she looked like a puppet made from a sock.

"Pepper needs to go out, don't you, boy?" The dog jumped up from where he lay at Gram's feet and ran to the door, slapping his tail against the wall.

I opened the kitchen door and he headed directly for the car, whining at the sound of Mama's sobbing. Their chorus about broke my heart.

"I'm sorry, I'm sorry." She repeated this apology, a mantra to some unknown listener, rocking her body in a rhythm to match her wails, unaware of me watching her.

Pepper scratched frantically at the car door. I took hold of his collar and dragged him back to the house. Gram sat slumped at the kitchen table, her head resting on her arms.

"Don't worry," said Sherry. "She's not dead." She stood at the counter chopping onions and celery. Water boiled over the edge of a pot of potatoes. "She's exhausted." She lowered the flame under the pot.

Gram was plain worn out. We roused her and said it was time for bed, but she insisted on staying close to Mama. We compromised and settled her on the couch in the living room. Sherry covered her with one of her own quilts, a log-cabin pattern of blues and reds. Gram reminded me of a baby, with her pink skin and thinning hair. I kissed her forehead and tucked the quilt under her chin.

"I can handle the picnic food," said Sherry. She brushed my bangs off my brow and managed a weak smile. "Go polish your fingernails or something."

I was too worn down to argue with her, so I took the Coke she offered me and climbed the back stairs two at a time. Pausing outside Daddy's room, I heard his snores. How could he sleep?

I threw open the door and marched over to his bed. "Daddy, wake up," I said into his ear.

A thundering snore ended with a snort. He sat up and shielded his eyes from the bedside light with his hand. "Ellen?" he said, mistaking me for Mama.

"It's Buddy, and I want to know why you're sleeping when Mama is still in the car. Don't you care about anybody but yourself?"

"Let me get my bearings. I must have been tired. I fell asleep as soon as my head hit the pillow." He leaned back against the headboard. "I do care, Buddy. You know your mama has her bad days, but I bet by Monday, she'll be looking for another place to volunteer."

"This time is different." Saying it made it real. Until that very moment I had held out hope, wished on stars, did all those things people do when they're desperate. I recalled how Mama looked all hunched and pulled into herself and in an instant I knew she was lost to us as surely as I knew Booth was dead and never coming home.

Daddy took hold of my hand. "It won't do any good to set up camp outside the car. She'll come out when she's ready. When your mama makes up her mind, there's no changing it."

I pushed his hand away. "We'll pull her out if we need to, but you have to help me find the extra key to the car."

He sighed and flapped his lips. "I have no idea where it could be. She's got drawers filled with extras of everything. Buttons, seashells, keys. I wouldn't know where to begin looking."

He slumped down on his pillow hill; my hands trembled with the urge to yank his pillow from behind his neck and pummel some sense into him.

"Trust me, Buddy. Your mama just needs time to collect herself. Don't treat her like a child." He closed his eyes and rolled onto his side.

I slammed his bedroom door hard enough to

rattle the mirror above Mama's dresser. From below, I heard the clang of pots being slammed about and detected the scent of fried onions. Feeling my way along the dark hall, I bumped into Gram's suitcase set outside the spare room. I opened the door and scooted the case across the hardwood floor. It struck the footboard of the bed and fell on its side.

"Everything okay up there?" yelled Sherry.

"It's just me tossing things around," I shouted down the stairs, but she had already gone back to her cooking, stopping long enough to tune to WKLM on the radio. The voice of Patsy Cline singing "Walkin' After Midnight" drifted up the stairs.

Booth's room was next to mine. I opened his door; light from the fish tank spilled across the soft green carpet like moonlight on a pond. His fish swam between the plastic plants and through an opening in an iridescent mountain. The bottom feeder I had bought him for his last birthday darted along the gravel scavenging for food.

I missed my brother. He was seven when I was born, already in school. My mother told me he'd wrapped one of his old baby rattles in freezer paper he'd finger-painted in blue and red, and placed it in my cradle the day they brought me home from the hospital.

After Booth died, Mama took over his room. She used his desk to do her paperwork for school and to pay the household bills. She said Daddy's fly-fishing stuff made it impossible to find anything in the den, but I think she liked being alone with the door shut tight surrounded by Booth's things. His football, basketball, and baseball trophies and plaques covered one wall. The shelves above his desk held his favorite books. I fingered a copy of *My Friend Flicka*, then returned it to its place between *Call of the Wild* and *Tom Sawyer*.

The flannel quilt made of blue plaid squares that Gram had sewed for his tenth birthday covered the foot of his bed. A copy of *All Quiet on the Western Front*, his place marked with a ticket stub from the Music Hall, lay on his bedside table.

I searched through the drawers of the scratched maple desk and found a small satin box filled with Chinese worry dolls. Beneath the dolls lay three keys. One looked like the extra key to the Buick. I pocketed the other two just in case.

CHAPTER FOUR

*T*HE KITCHEN stood empty; I stepped outside and found Sherry sitting on the porch glider smoking, the ember of her cigarette glowed bright, then darkened like a blinking signal light. Through the porch window, I spied Pepper curled up at the end of the couch next to Gram. He raised his head and stared at me; I motioned for him to stay.

"What are you up to, Buddy? Can't sleep?" Sherry patted the cushion next to her. "Come sit by me."

"In a minute. I want to get a drink."

"Ellen's not coming in till she's ready." Sherry could always read my mind.

"I know, but I've got to try. It doesn't seem right, leaving her there. It's like seeing a wreck and driving on by."

Sherry stubbed out her cigarette and peeled back the wrapper of a Three Musketeers bar. "Suit yourself."

I walked across the front lawn, jammed my hand in my pocket and squeezed the keys; their points bit into my palms like puppy teeth.

The first key I tried opened the locked door. I slipped into the car and sat on the seat where Mama lay gulping air. My right hand rested on the space between us.

"Mama," I whispered. "I'm here."

A touch, light as a butterfly, grazed my fingers. That simple gesture took me back to when I was little and Mama would come into my room at the first roll of thunder to sit on the edge of my narrow bed. As I hid beneath my sheet, she spoke to me of clear cloudless nights when we could see every star in the sky.

"Don't be afraid, Buddy," she would tell me in a voice soft as cobwebs. "A storm is nothing but the angels clearing away the dust so the stars can shine their brightest."

When she grew tired and I refused to let her go, she would lie on the floor next to my bed, reach up and feather my hand with her bright red fingernails. If I caught her crawling from my room, she returned and stayed until I fell asleep.

Sitting next to Mama in Daddy's Buick, I tried to comfort her. "Are you all right, Mama?"

She struggled to sit up. "I'm sorry if I upset you, Buddy. I don't know what's happening to me."

"It's just one of your spells. It will pass. Isn't that what you always tell me when I'm having a bad day? It will pass."

"Maybe I was wrong. Besides, things are different this time. Bad days pass, but I'm having a bad life."

"Is that why you kept saying you were sorry? What do you have to be sorry about, Mama?"

She stared through the front windshield of the car as if she could find the answer to my question written on the side of the house. "I was in the pickle aisle at the Winn-Dixie this afternoon, reading my list, and then I got lost somehow, couldn't figure out where I was going. I started wandering up and down the aisles just throwing things into my cart."

"I know. You got three jars of mustard. And five kinds of pickles."

A small smile tugged at the corners of her mouth. "I didn't have enough money to pay for everything. Brenda, that big-haired girl who works the express line, offered to loan me ten dollars, but I said no, thank you, I could do without the rib roast and T-bones and put them back, not remembering why I picked them up in the first place."

"You were upset, so you shopped to make yourself feel better, like Ginger's mom."

"Buddy, when Ceci goes on a binge, she buys herself shoes and jewelry, not a side of beef."

Mama came out of her slump and sat up straight. "I paid the girl for my groceries, wheeled the cart outside, and didn't know what to do next. There I was in the middle of the Winn-Dixie parking lot with Billy Perkins loading my groceries into the wagon, telling me to have a happy Fourth of July. I asked myself, what am I doing shopping for a

Fourth of July celebration? What have I got to celebrate? I don't deserve to be happy."

She took a deep breath as if she were about to dive under water. "I tipped him a quarter, got in the car and drove around that lot looking for a way out."

"And then what, Mama? What happened next?" Something told me I had to keep her talking, keep her alert.

"I don't exactly know. I found myself sitting behind the Music Hall. I didn't even check to see what was playing. Just slapped down my money and told Wanda to give me the biggest box of popcorn they sell and two boxes of Good and Plenty."

Mama's lips trembled; she pressed them tight together as if she were trying to swallow bitter-tasting medicine. I opened my eyes wide, to understand her better.

"Don't you see, Buddy, I went there to get away from my worries. For once in my life I said, Let everybody take care of themselves. And then I'm sitting there minding my own business, watching Elizabeth Taylor sashaying around in one glamorous dress after another, eating my popcorn, relaxing, and before I knew it, the credits were rolling on the screen and the lights came on."

"And that's when you attached yourself to Junior Nevins?" The image still made my stomach lurch.

Mama shuddered. "I'm sorry, Buddy. I never meant to embarrass you. Junior Nevins would not listen to me. He told me I would have to buy another ticket if I wanted to stay for the next show. Why didn't he see I couldn't go back out there?"

"Out where?"

She clamped her hands into fists. "Here, in the real world, where there are no happy endings. Where children die the minute you turn your back for even a second."

I knew where this was headed. Booth again. After two years, he was still all she thought about. Oh, she fixed meals with good cuts of meat, two vegetables and Rice Krispies treats for dessert, but she was going through the motions. Even in death, my brother still commanded her attention.

She had once told me she saw him everywhere. There were days I believe she could not see me, clear in front of her face.

"It wasn't your fault that Booth died. You're a good mother." I patted her back.

"No, I'm not. If I were a good mother he'd still be alive."

It was not news to me Mama took that original-sin stuff literally, but how could she blame herself for Booth's death, when he was five hundred miles from home when he died?

"He died in a car wreck, Mama."

"He didn't have a mark on him." She fingered her neck.

I heard my daddy explain to a customer who inquired about the accident how Booth's neck had snapped in two when a Cadillac Eldorado plowed into the Ford sedan he was riding in with his room-mate. His roommate lived for two days.

The officer at the scene testified in court that the man driving the car who caused the accident couldn't walk a straight line when he got out of his car. "Mr. Dinfrey was as drunk as a skunk," he volunteered to the judge before the defense attorney could object.

"It wasn't your fault he died. How can you even think that? A drunk driver killed him."

"You don't understand, Buddy." She stroked the side of my face with her hand. "I loved you and Booth so much, but I kept waiting for God to take you away. Just like he took away my brother Tommy when he was five."

"Mama, how can you feel guilty?"

"Because I didn't let Booth take his car to school. I thought he'd be safer riding the bus."

"Lots of parents don't let their kids take cars to school. And even if he had his car, he still would have died." Daddy told people at the wake, no one could have survived that accident.

Mama looked toward the barn set behind the house. "Booth loved that car. If he'd had his car, he'd be alive."

"That's the silliest thing I ever heard you say. Just because he never got a ticket doesn't mean he could save himself from some drunken idiot." I needed to get her mind off Booth. "Please, Mama, let's go in the house. We have to get up early tomorrow for the picnic."

She shook her head no. "I can't face those people."

"Everyone loves you. You can pretend you're feeling poorly and lie in the hammock. Gram and Sherry and I will do the serving. And Tess will be here in the morning. She can handle anything."

Even as Mama reached out to me, I felt her slipping away. "Listen to me, Buddy. Something's wrong. It's not like a broken leg that everyone can see and say, 'Hey, Ellen, hope you get better.' I hurt so bad, and I want the pain to stop."

"I'll take care of you, Mama. Whatever hurts, we'll fix it together. Remember how you used to bring me chicken-noodle soup and comic books when I was sick in bed? I can do that. We'll go to the picture show every day and see funny movies with Cary Grant and those swimming movies with Esther Williams. The ones where she dives under water and never gets her hair wet. We'll get Jujubes stuck in our teeth and pretend we need a dentist real bad and . . ."

She kissed my cheek. "I think Esther Williams is retired. Please don't ask me to try, Buddy. I don't have the strength. You'll be better off without me. You'll get along just fine. I deserve to be alone, some place like Moodus Meadows, where I can't hurt anyone ever again."

The muscles of her face tightened into a smile. With a trembling hand, she reached out and tweaked my nose. "You were born old, Buddy. Don't try to hold the world on your shoulders. It will drive you nuts. Now, be a good girl for Mama. Go get your daddy and tell him I need a ride to Moodus Meadows."

CHAPTER FIVE

MAYBE IT was the look on my face, but the next time I woke Daddy, he reached over to the bedside phone and called Dr. Gates. "Ellen's jumped over the moon," is how he put it, and Doc Gates told him to bring her to Moodus Meadows. No sense waiting another day.

It made me sad to think of Mama living inside one of those red-brick buildings surrounded by a towering black wrought-iron fence. I passed Moodus Meadows on my way to school; once I heard a cry from somewhere inside, a cry from so deep it came out as a howl.

I usually crossed the street so I wouldn't have to walk too close to the gate, afraid someone might snatch me up and lock me inside a room where no one would ever find me. Kind of like keeping your hands under the covers so the monsters under the bed can't get you.

Moodus is a small town, not grand enough to have its own mental hospital. According to Gram, Moodus Meadows was a catchall rest home for people too well for the hospital and too sick to go home, a last resort.

"Please stay here, Mama. Things will get better. I promise." Mama and I stood under the red maple in our front yard. Out of the corner of my eye, I watched Daddy stumble down the steps. He moved toward us, his head down, his shoulders dragged forward as if he were being pulled against his will by a towline.

He took hold of my hand. "Call your aunt Tess and ask her to come stay with you."

Sherry stood with one arm wrapped around Gram, easing her closer with each breath she took. Mama's suitcase sat on the ground, an exclamation point to the scene before me.

"Time to get this show on the road. You be good." Mama gave me a hug. I sensed her calmness, as if making the decision to leave had released her from a burden, given her a second wind, something to propel her to the finish line.

"Don't go, Mama. Please stay." I reached around her thin middle and clasped my hands together, deluding myself that if I held on to her long enough, she'd change her mind.

Mama wriggled from my grasp and kissed me one last time. Gram insisted on going along, saying Mama was still her daughter, and she had every right to be with her. Daddy asked me to stay behind in case someone called needing a prescription. It was probably a ruse to spare me the humiliation of checking Mama into Moodus Meadows.

Sherry took me aside and whispered in my ear. "If I were you, I'd get out your softball bat, then find the biggest pillow in the house and beat the stuffing out of it." She eyed me to make sure I had heard her right.

"Okay, maybe I will," I said as I stiffened my jaw to keep it from quivering.

Maybe I'd beat some sense into Mama. She wouldn't have left Booth. How could she abandon me? Weren't mothers supposed to fight to be with their children? If she was so afraid God was going to take me away when her back was turned, why didn't she stick around to keep an eye on me? It would serve her right if I disappeared.

The Buick pulled away; there I stood, the last person on earth, the one the aliens left behind. Too young, too small, a person of no consequence. I watched the taillights' red glow shrink to dots of light. One wink and they were gone.

Everything in the house reminded me of Mama. The stacks of magazines piled high in the corners of the rooms, the yellowed newspaper clippings tacked to anything soft enough to hold a pin—they told of a woman who couldn't bear to discard a scrap of paper for fear it might contain the answers she would need to save the world.

I knew she loved me as sure as I knew I had fly-away brown hair that would never curl. But she was not thinking about love when she dumped three sets of underwear, two cotton shifts, a handful of socks, a toothbrush, and a black plastic comb into a takeout bag from the Crazy Chicken.

"She's not herself," Gram had said when she placed Mama's belongings into a suitcase to save the family's reputation.

If she wasn't herself, who was she? Where did the real Mama go; where was she hiding? When Booth died, she told me he'd gone to heaven. Mama was here on earth, but she was dead inside, her heart turned to stone. I wished I knew where to look for her.

I dragged Pepper from his bed on the couch to keep me company and shooed him out the kitchen door. We ran through the pasture to the barn, the high, wet grass painting my legs with dew. Pepper startled as I slid open the barn door, his loose skin drawing back from his ribcage.

"It's okay, Pepper. Come on." I tugged at his collar, but he planted his fat rump on the dirt floor and whined. "Be a baby," I said, and let him be.

I felt for the light switch, the barn wood rough beneath my fingers. Pepper whimpered and crawled backward until he lay half in and half out of the barn.

I flipped the light switch, and a row of cobweb-covered lights came on and cast a soft glow over us. Pepper growled at the canvas-covered mound stationed between the stalls.

"It's only a car," I said aloud, and yanked the tarp from its moorings. The dusty gray cloth slid to the floor, puddling around Booth's turquoise-and-white Chevy Bel Air convertible, the overhead light bouncing off the chrome trim.

"Come on," I urged. Pepper moved closer. "Get in, boy." I leaned over and patted the rear seat where Pepper had sat when Booth drove us to the store for coffee-ice-cream sodas. The day he left for college, he promised to drive me to the Grand Canyon the next summer.

Pepper inched forward, sniffing the still air, seduced by the familiar smell of Booth's car. He entered cautiously, one paw at a time. Settling himself on the cool upholstery, he let out a sigh as if he were glad to be home.

I climbed into the driver's seat, pulled the keys from my pocket and examined them under the dashboard light. The key to the Bel Air looked familiar in my hand. I leaned back, closed my eyes, and the memory of another summer night settled on my mind.

It was a night in August just before Booth left for college. We'd picnicked by the river that day. The whole family, including Gram, Tess, and Sherry, had feasted on cold chicken, homemade potato salad, and angel-food cake topped with fresh strawberries. Booth and I swam in the river, while Sherry sunned herself on the dock. Mama and Daddy played horseshoes with Tess and Gram. It was a perfect day. No one wanted to leave; we stayed past sunset, toasting marshmallows over a campfire.

Booth opened going-away gifts; a new patchwork quilt from Gram; a toiletry case from Tess; Foster Grant sunglasses from Sherry to make him look cool; spending money and preaddressed stamped postcards from Mama and Daddy so he'd write once a week. I wrapped a framed photo of the two of us sitting in the Bel Air.

Mama and Daddy went to bed as soon as we got home. Booth's friend Henry came by and the two of them took off to go cruising Main Street. I envied him being able to go out late at night.

It was past midnight when Booth came into my room.

"Get up, Buddy," he said as he nudged me. I lay in the top bunk, unable to sleep because of my sunburn. I reached over and snapped on the wall light.

"What's going on?"

Booth's blue eyes shone like sparkly sapphires against his tan skin. He was still dressed in his cutoff jeans and a white T-shirt.

"I'll be leaving for school in a few weeks and I thought maybe you'd like a driving lesson."

I sat up so fast I bumped my head on the sloped ceiling. "Would I ever. Mama's going to make me wait until I'm forty."

He laughed and mussed my hair. "Yeah, Mama worries more than a hen in a foxhole. So you can't tell her," he warned me. "If you keep it a secret, we can practice whenever I'm home from school. Then when you turn sixteen, you can tell Mama you already know how to drive, so she'll have to let you get your license. It's that simple."

Nothing was ever simple with Mama, but I couldn't pass up the chance to learn to drive. I pulled on shorts and a shirt over my shorty pajamas, then slipped into yesterday's socks and tied up my tennis shoes. We tiptoed down the hall and listened at the last door to the sound of Mama and Daddy's snores.

"Are you sure this is okay?" I asked Booth as we let ourselves out the kitchen door, careful to shoo Pepper outside so he wouldn't start to howl and wake up the dead.

He pulled on one of my braids. "Trust me, Buddy. You're talking to a big-shot college man."

"Yeah, yeah, I know, you're going away to school and all the girls will fall in love with you. Just remember I know all your secrets, like how you fart in your sleep. That's what I'm going to call you. Booth Mullens, the Night Farter."

"Just for that, I'm going to put worms on your head." He reached down, picked up a night crawler and chased me to the barn. Pepper ran alongside me, nipping at my floppy socks.

I collapsed on the floor of the barn, rubbing at a stitch in my side. "Drop that worm on me and I'll scream!"

He dropped his hands to his sides. "Okay, I'll

give you a reprieve this time. Come on and get in."
He motioned for me to get into the driver's seat of
his car. Pepper jumped over the front seat and took
his place in the back.

"Maybe this isn't such a good idea. What if I
crash your car?" Booth had used all his savings from
six years of working a paper route and two summers
of lifeguarding at the town pool to buy the Bel Air.

He laughed and gave me a gentle punch in the
arm. "You're not going to crash. I've seen you drive
the tractor. You have good reflexes, Buddy. Besides,
you're not a little kid anymore."

I don't know what pleased me more, driving the
Bel Air or hearing those words from Booth. "Okay.
What do I do first?"

"First, we better boost you up so you can see
over the steering wheel." He reached into the back
for a blanket, which he folded into a cushion for me
to sit on. "Now, turn the key in the ignition."

He passed me the key; it felt as precious as a
nugget of gold in my hand.

"Make sure the car is in gear." He placed his
hand on mine and showed me how to shift.

We moved the stick through first gear, second, third, reverse, neutral. Then he taught me how to work the clutch. After I'd practiced, I backed the car from the barn, popping the clutch three times before I got the hang of it.

With the top down and me at the wheel, we bumped and lurched over the hillocks in the field, the radio on so low you could hear the tree toads singing along to the music.

"I did it," I said in amazement as I slowed the car to a stop in the middle of the clearing. "Mama will never believe this. She thinks I'm still a baby."

"If Mama had her way, she'd never let us out of her sight. I know she loves us, but she's a worrier. You can't let her wear you down. Stand up to her, Buddy, or you'll be living at home when you're forty-five."

"Yeah, with Mama still driving me to the movies and picking out my clothes."

Booth laughed and turned the radio dial until he found a station playing a Buddy Holly song. He leaned back against the seat. I did the same.

"I'm going to miss you when you leave."

"You're not getting mushy, are you?"

"Nah, why would I get mushy over a night farter?"

"Look, Buddy, I know that it gets tough around here when Mama has her spells, but it's not like I'm going away forever. I'll be home at Thanksgiving and Christmas. And don't forget the Grand Canyon, we're going there next summer."

"What if Mama says I can't go?"

"Then we'll leave at night when she's sleeping and send her postcards from Arizona."

I knew he meant it. Mama thought Booth was perfect, but he did things behind her back any chance he got. Like the time he told her he was going camping with his friends, when they really went to New Orleans where they drank beer and saw naked ladies dancing in a club.

I imagined us taking off for the Grand Canyon in the dead of night, leaving a note behind, telling Mama not to worry about us, even though I knew she would.

"It's going to be lonely without you to talk to. You can always make Mama smile, even on a bad day. I'll write to you," I promised. "We can make plans for our trip."

"I'd like that," he said. "I may not have much time to write back, but I'll be thinking about you."

"You'll be too busy romancing all those Yankee girls to think about me."

"How could I forget about my pesky little sister? If it gets too bad, call Sherry. Tell her, Sherry, you better come rescue me. She'll do it; that girl is wild."

"But how will I know you're thinking about me if I don't hear from you?"

"Look, Buddy." Booth pointed to the night sky. "It's the Big Dipper, watching over you. Whenever you get lonely or things get tough around here, come outside and look up at the sky. I'll do the same every night, so when you see the Big Dipper, you can be sure I'm thinking about you."

Two years later, on the night Mama left, I sat in Booth's car and wondered if anything or anyone had ever watched over us. If it were true, then why did Booth die and why did Mama lose herself to grief?

I sat up tall, opened my eyes and inserted the key

into the ignition, turning it hard. "Here goes nothing," I said to Pepper.

The engine sprang to life; I suspected Mama might have been starting it up, just in case. I lowered the convertible top; Pepper flinched and flattened himself on the seat. Imaging Booth's hand on mine, guiding me every step of the way, I shifted the car into reverse and the car slipped through the open doors. Pepper sat up; his ears waved like soft flags and wisps of my hair blew across my eyes as we sailed around the side of the barn.

We coasted to a stop in the middle of the field. I turned off the engine and climbed into the back to sit with Pepper; it was the seat I took when Booth, Pepper, Mama, and I went cruising. "I'll be copilot," Mama would shout as she raced to the car to claim her place.

That night, Pepper and I sat alone in Booth's car. Pepper leaned against me, the warmth of his bony head easing my pain, connecting me to someone. I will not cry, I told myself, and looking up to keep my tears from escaping, I saw the Big Dipper ablaze in the sky.

CHAPTER SIX

THE ABSENCE of my family made the time pass slowly. An hour felt like a lifetime. I kept hoping Mama would change her mind and realize she needed to be safe at home with her loved ones, instead of sleeping with strangers. Maybe Doc Gates would set her straight, give her a firm pat on the back and advise her to go home and get a good night's sleep. Surely she would trust the man who had brought her into the world.

I remembered Daddy told me to call Aunt Tess, but I couldn't bear the thought of having to tell her about Mama. Hours passed with no news. Pepper snored as he dozed on the braided rug in front of the fireplace. I should have gone with them, even if I had to hang onto the bumper of the car and get dragged all the way to the hospital. Mama needed me.

I turned on the radio for company and plopped myself into Daddy's La-Z-Boy. His reading glasses lay on top of a book about the Civil War. I pictured him at the hospital, patting the deep pockets of his trousers, then cursing himself for misplacing them again.

Pepper twitched in his sleep, startling himself awake. He came over to me, nudging my hand until I took the hint and massaged the bony ridge between his ears. "It's okay, boy," I reassured him.

I got up and turned off the radio. Pepper followed me from room to room, his nails clicking on the hardwood floors. We settled ourselves at the kitchen window, me in a chair, Pepper at my side, his nose pressed against the glass.

"Where are they, boy?" I looked into the darkness for the answer.

I was sharing a hot dog with Pepper when Sherry

burst through the kitchen door. She walked past me to the refrigerator smelling of cigarettes and peppermints.

"Well, Ellen's all settled. She's got herself a private room with a window overlooking a garden and a big-ass nurse watching her like a hawk. Suicide watch." Sherry helped herself to a bottle of cold ginger ale.

"They think Mama's going to kill herself?"

Sherry wrapped an arm around my shoulders. "She's going to be all right. Doc Gates says they keep an eye on every new patient for the first forty-eight hours."

"But Mama never said she wanted to die." Was that what she'd meant when she said everyone was better off without her? How could she even think that for a second?

Sherry flopped in the chair by the window and untied her shoes, the laces leaving imprints on her legs. "Buddy, what does she have to do, climb to the top of the tallest building in town and announce she's going to jump? Ellen needs help."

I didn't want to think about Mama killing

herself. Not that there is ever a good time to contemplate something so terrifying, but that night my mind was worn to a frazzle and couldn't begin to process any new information.

Instead of facing the truth, I changed the subject. "Is the hospital nice inside?" I imagined cracked green linoleum floors and mournful voices calling from darkened rooms. Except for Mama's room, where she would lie quiet on her narrow bed thinking about . . . me.

Sherry opened the ginger ale and offered me a sip. "Moodus Meadows isn't the Ritz, but I've stayed in worse places. It's clean and the other patients don't seem too crazy. At least not the ones I saw walking around." She shrugged her shoulders. "Of course, they probably keep the real bad ones locked up in padded rooms so they can't hurt themselves."

"That's not funny, Sherry."

"Sorry, Buddy, but you've got to lighten up. This is not the end of the world. At least Ellen's getting help. It's not bad inside, sort of like an emergency Holiday Inn."

Daddy and Gram came in before I could ask

Sherry if Mama had said anything about me, sent a message home for me to come see her in the morning. Daddy's face softened with relief when he heard Sherry had filled me in, sparing him the chore.

He hugged me gently. "Get some sleep, Buddy. You'll see, things will look better in the morning." Taking hold of Gram's arm, she let him help her up the stairs.

"Okay, Buddy, let's hit the hay." Sherry busied herself turning off the lights and locking up. I sniffed the stove for gas leaks the way Mama did every night before she went to bed.

Sherry was supposed to share the guest room with Gram, but when she opened the door, Gram's snores ripped through the air.

"I won't get a wink of sleep in there." She pulled the door closed. "I'll take Booth's room."

"No, you can't." I grabbed at her elbow to stop her. She pulled away from me and marched toward my brother's room. "Mama wouldn't like it."

Sherry turned and even in the dim light I could see her roll her eyes at me. "It's been long enough, Buddy. She treats that room like a museum. No wonder she cracked up." She threw open the door, turned on the light and walked over to Booth's dresser, examining the clay dish he had made in first grade, still filled with change and paper clips.

"I don't know Sherry, it doesn't seem right letting you take over his room, going behind her back."

Sherry sighed and put her arm through mine. "Hush up, Buddy, I won't desecrate the shrine, but I'm going to talk to Ellen as soon as she's steady on her feet. Someone has to make her see this is unnatural. If a stranger came into this house right now, he'd think Booth was out with his friends instead of dead in the ground for two years."

I picked up the box of Chinese worry dolls and lifted the lid slowly, as if it might explode.

"What's that?" Sherry grabbed the box from me. "Oh, I remember these. We bought them on our trip to New York City."

"Let's go to bed," I said, taking the box from her and jamming it in my pocket. "I'm tired."

That was a lie. At that moment I thought I might never sleep again, like one of those people you read about in the magazines at the grocery store checkout. But I couldn't stand to be in Booth's room one more second. It seemed haunted, not by my brother, but by Mama. What was she doing, what was she thinking about, during all those hours she spent in there alone with the door shut?

Sherry weighed the pros and cons of sleeping with me or sleeping with Gram and decided bunking with me was the lesser of two evils. "Looks like we're roomies tonight, kiddo."

My room stood just as I had left it that afternoon; copies of *Seventeen* magazine lay scattered over my bed; my favorite blue shirt hung from my chair, waiting to be ironed. Buddy Holly smiled at me from a poster on my wall. In the space of an evening, my world had been blown to bits. How had my room escaped the disaster? My dresser should have been turned upside down, my clothes up in flames.

I lay on the floor, the carpet scratching my legs, observing Sherry slather Pond's Cold Cream on her face and remove her makeup with pink tissues. She did this slowly with small strokes, as carefully as an artist restoring a masterpiece. Satisfied with her work, she tossed the used tissues into the wastebasket, pulled on a nightshirt and sprayed herself with White Shoulders cologne.

I threw my stuffed animals from my bed to the floor and gestured to Sherry. "You can have the lower bunk."

She tossed a copy of *Glamour* magazine on the bed. "Thanks. I'm too old to sleep up there."

I put on last night's pajamas and settled myself on the top bunk, the box of worry dolls clutched in one hand. The bunk beds had been a present for my sixth birthday. The first time I slept up there, Mama had placed sofa cushions on the floor, "Just in case."

Sherry yawned and dropped her magazine to the floor. "I'm beat."

"Me too." I turned out the wall lamp.

"Sherry, are you awake?"

"Uh-huh."

"What are you thinking about?"

"I'm remembering how Hazel always sent me to bed early when I was having a bad day. She promised everything would feel better in the morning."

"The only thing that will make me feel better is waking up to the sound of Mama rattling some pots and pans in the kitchen."

"I'll make a racket for you, Buddy. Will that help?"

"It helps that you're here."

"Hey, that's what buddies are for. I'm going to sleep now, but wake me up if you need to talk." Sherry didn't say anything after that, but I heard the swish of the satin comforter as she tried to get comfortable in a strange bed.

Pepper whimpered in his sleep, as he lay curled on the overstuffed chair near the window. All I could think about was Mama alone in her bed. Was she thinking of me? Did I matter to her anymore?

★ ★ ★

As I lay in bed, unable to sleep, I tried to pinpoint when it had all started, that moment Mama's sadness turned her inside out. After Booth died, she had tried so hard to cheer up everyone else, she hadn't given herself a chance to heal.

If I hadn't been so sad myself, maybe I would have noticed sooner. Missing my brother came in waves of sadness. In good times I almost forgot he was gone for good, days I could imagine he was still away at school pursuing his dreams. Then something simple would happen; I'd discover a book he might enjoy and I'd start to write to tell him about it, remembering too late he wasn't there to tell.

During those first months I tried to keep his face alive in my mind, thumbing through photo albums searching for a hint, a foreshadowing of what was to come. Mama held up well at the wake and in the weeks that followed she asked me to go to the movies or to the diner for chiliburgers. Sherry came by and played her new records for me. Daddy begged for help at the drugstore.

I wanted to be left alone. Some days I'd sit on the couch in the living room, my feet pulled close to my chest, my body wedged into the soft cushions. *American Bandstand* played on the TV, everyone happy and dancing to "Rock Around the Clock."

My friend Ginger and I used to wish we could be on that show, dancing in front of the cameras.

After Booth died, I prayed to be like a dandelion, to turn into a puffball and be scattered to the wind. Numb with grief, I remained still, waiting to disappear.

The night Mama left us, I lay in the bed above Sherry, feeling betrayed. First Booth had died and made me an only child, and now Mama was gone.

Matching my breathing to Sherry's, I promised myself to get Mama out of Moodus Meadows and bring her home where she belonged.

CHAPTER SEVEN

𝒯HE NEXT morning Sherry dragged me out of bed at seven. I wanted to stay there wrapped in the tangle of sheets for the rest of my life, but she convinced me Tess would never forgive us if we missed seeing her ride in the parade.

Daddy and Gram stayed behind to attend to the picnic. Daddy promised to call and check on Mama, but I wanted to do it myself. I was reaching for the phone when Sherry called to me from the porch.

"Come on, Buddy. Hurry up or we'll miss the start of the parade." Sherry wore a pair of red short-shorts with a white cotton off-the-shoulder blouse and white ballet slippers. Gold metallic ribbons resembling sparklers held her hair back from her face.

I watched the house as we drove away. Even though Mama wasn't there, it seemed wrong to be heading off to a parade. Sherry fiddled with the radio dial until she found a channel playing Brenda Lee singing "I'm Sorry." She informed me that her lipstick was Cherries in the Snow as she applied a thick coat while looking in the rearview mirror.

I sat next to her in the front seat of the Impala, picking at the threads of my cutoff jeans. Sherry sped to town, convinced anyone who could give her a ticket was probably lining up to be in the parade.

"Where'd you get that shirt?" She eyed my white cotton top, its sleeves rolled up, its long tails hanging limp against my legs.

"It's one of Daddy's. He said the collar's too frayed to wear for good anymore, so I could have it." It still held the scent of the spray starch Mama used when she ironed.

"Next week I'm taking you to JCPenney for

some serious shopping. I get a discount, so you'll save real big."

"I don't need anything. My clothes are fine."

Sherry took her eyes off the road long enough to give me the once over. "Maybe for summer, but we've got to get you fixed up for school. You're going to high school, Buddy."

"It's not a big deal."

"That's where you're wrong. High school can change your life."

That was not what I wanted to hear on the morning after my Mama checked herself into the loony bin. More change. Why couldn't I stay thirteen forever, live at home with my dog and my books and let everyone else grow old around me?

We heard the sound of the marching band tuning up as soon as we turned the corner from Broadway onto Main Street. Buildings draped with red-white-and-blue bunting stood proud, their windows clean and sparkling in the morning sun, each displayed an American flag waving from a bracket. People wearing loud summer clothes and all sorts of funny hats dragged folding chairs and pushed baby buggies along clogged sidewalks trying to get a good place to view the parade. Sherry slowed the Impala to a crawl. We parked behind the drugstore in the spot marked PHARMACIST.

"This place is a zoo." Sherry steered me in the direction of the firehouse. I inhaled the spice-and-flower smell of her new scent, Arpège.

We found Tess making last-minute adjustments to her costume. "This thing must weigh ten pounds," she said as she straightened the white wig on her head. "At least I don't have to wear a beard." She pointed to a tall, thin man dressed as Uncle Sam sporting a beard thick as cotton candy.

"You look good, Aunt Tess." I fingered the long striped cotton skirt of her dress. I remembered her standing on a chair while Mama stood beneath her pinning up the hem.

"Where is everybody?" Tess looked behind us for the rest of the family.

I opened my mouth to speak, but Sherry slipped in front of me, stepping on my foot in the process. "They're busy with the picnic. You know how crazy it gets at the last minute. Hazel always thinks there won't be enough food and Herb worries about the grills getting set up in time."

"You broke my toe," I complained as I massaged my foot. Sherry ignored me and smiled at a good-looking fireman hitching up the float to a tractor. He tipped his dark blue hat; the silver badge glinted in the sun.

"What about Ellen, she never misses a parade." Tess swiped at a rivulet of sweat running from her forehead.

"Ellen ate something that didn't agree with her. She was still on the toilet when we left." Sherry gave me the look, the one that said to go along with whatever she said.

Sherry, Daddy, and Gram thought it best to let Tess have her day in the sun before telling her about Mama, but I knew we'd pay the price for shutting her out. Tess liked to be included in everybody's business, and I didn't want to be around when she found out she'd been deceived.

I looked for my friend Ginger in the crowd. Since she was coming late, we planned to meet at the firehouse after the parade where the firemen handed out as much free ice cream and pop as you could handle. Ginger was one of my two best friends. She was what I called my congenital best friend—someone assigned to me from birth. We had been born two days apart in the same hospital, Ginger being the older one and bossing me from the start. Our mamas had been friends since fifth grade. Ginger sparkled like a diamond; next to her I looked as dull as an unpolished stone. Sometimes I wondered if she would have chosen me for a friend on her own.

I imagined us walking together on our first day of high school, and pictured Ginger stopping at the front door, turning to me with that beautiful smile of hers and saying, "Why, Buddy, this is where we part company. Surely you didn't expect me to hang around with you in high school."

She was born beautiful, with naturally wavy blond hair, eyes the color of blue irises in spring and the delicate build of a ballerina. She lived in a Victorian house by the river and never went out looking less than perfect.

My other best friend, Verna Kaye Sanford,

hovered in the background of my life, a shadow. Put in charge of her younger brothers and sisters because of her mama's polio, she came and went from school, learning the best she could with the kindness of teachers and my careful notes. We'd been in the same class since kindergarten and became friends when she offered to share her crayons with me. She always let me use the red one first.

I didn't expect to see Verna at the parade. She'd be busy at home caring for her mama. Ginger and Verna mixed as well as a hen and a fox. Not that Ginger would say anything mean to Verna, but I suspected Verna's circumstances made Ginger uncomfortable. Maybe she thought you could catch poverty by standing too close to it.

The tractor's engine came to life. "Here goes nothing," said Tess. Uncle Sam reached down and helped her up on the float. They sat on a bench with a background of a map of the United States made from crepe-paper carnations.

"Want to be in the parade?" The fireman who'd been making eyes at Sherry patted the seat next to him on the tractor.

She looked at me and ruffled my hair. "How 'bout it, Buddy? Want to go for a ride?"

I could tell by the way she gazed at that guy, whose name was Darren McCoy, that she wanted to sit beside him in the worst way.

"No, thanks, I've got to meet Ginger."

"Okay, see you back here when it's over." Sherry squeezed as close to Darren as icing on a cake, adjusting her sunglasses and waving to Tess, who worked the crowd, throwing candy from a bucket.

Usually Mama and I watched the parade from the apartment above the drugstore. It was mostly a catchall place for out-of-season displays and extra cartons of hot-water bottles and shaving cream, but Mama had furnished it with a table and chairs and a small desk for doing paperwork.

Moving through the crowd took some doing. A woman banged against my leg with a folding chair. I felt in my pocket for my keys. I'd had enough of the heat and rude people, so I headed for the drugstore.

I let myself in through the back door, careful to lock it behind me. Sherry hadn't given me a chance to have breakfast, and my stomach rumbled with hunger. The store felt refreshingly cool and smelled sweet from the peppermint soaps and boxes of candy stacked on the shelves.

If anyone saw me in there, they'd be banging on the door to be let in, thirsty for a cherry Coke or a root-beer float. Stooping behind the counter, I made myself a coffee ice-cream soda with extra syrup and ice cream and carried it upstairs where the air stirred warm and dusty.

The red-and-chrome Formica table and chairs hunkered against the front window with its view of Main Street. I dusted off the table with my arm and perched on one of the vinyl chairs. It took some doing, but I managed to get the window open to let in some fresh air. The sounds of "When the Saints Come Marching In," heavy on the tuba, wafted up to me. Members of the high-school marching band stepped in place beneath the window, and I ducked my head, like a burglar caught in the act, when the drummer looked up and smiled at me.

If Mama were there, we would have been hurling streamers out the window, and singing along with the band. But she was in Moodus Meadows, and I doubted she remembered what day it was.

"Buddy, let me in." Ginger stood on the sidewalk below waving her straw satchel at me.

"Hush up. Come around to the back door." Watching the parade with Ginger was not part of my plan, but it was too late to hide. I ran down the stairs and let her in.

"I couldn't believe when I saw you in the window. I thought we were going to meet at the firehouse."

"After the parade, I said."

Ginger went over to the soda fountain and helped herself to a ginger ale and a handful of licorice whips. "This is even better. We'll be able to see everything from upstairs. Come on, we're going to miss the football team."

I followed her up the stairs, watching the dizzying motion of the ruffles on her pink blouse and matching shorts. Her tanned legs looked sleek as silk. Ginger had started shaving in sixth grade and never left a nick. Most of the time the skin on my legs looked fuzzy, like the skin on peaches.

My coffee soda had melted into soup, but I drank it anyway, being lightheaded with hunger. Ginger took great pains to dust her chair before balancing on the edge to wait for a glimpse of the Moodus High football team. A minute later they appeared in their red-and-white uniforms, shoulders three feet wide with padding, helmets tucked under their arms like crowns of royalty.

"Here they come," squealed Ginger as she spotted the team make the turn onto Main Street. "That's Jimmy Vance, the quarterback at the front. Isn't he the dreamiest boy you've ever seen?"

"He's okay."

Ginger took a bite of licorice whip. "He's more than okay, Buddy. Why, if he were to ask me out, I think I'd die."

"Don't you think he's a little old for you? He must be at least sixteen."

She rolled her eyes at me. "Buddy, we're going to be freshmen in September, and no respectable freshman girl would date a freshman boy. If you're going to do that you might as well stay in grammar school. I mean what is the point of finally getting into high school if not to date older boys? Preferably ones with cars."

"Mama would never let me go on a date in a car." As soon as I said the words I wondered if Mama would even be around when school started. Or if she would care about anything I did. I could run wild, wear tight skirts with slits up the sides and white-frosted lipstick.

"Are you listening to me?" Ginger waved a hand in front of my face.

"Yes, I heard you. We can't date freshmen boys."

"Not if you want to get off on the right foot. We are going to have an incredible year." She sucked up the ginger ale through the straw, leaving a bit at the bottom. "Just follow my lead, Buddy, and you'll do fine."

I wanted to believe her, the part about me being fine, but it had nothing to do with boys. What if Mama were still in Moodus Meadows come September? More than anything I wished to have her at school sitting in her guidance office dispensing advice the way Daddy dispensed medicine, and having lunch with Tess every day, laughing behind closed doors.

"Let's get to the firehouse before it gets too crowded." The sooner I got home the better. My skin tightened every time I imagined Mama all alone in her room at Moodus Meadows. I needed to talk to her. I picked up our empty glasses and carried them downstairs, Ginger at my heels.

She read greeting cards in the display rack while I washed and dried the glasses. "Buddy, how come you're here by yourself?"

I was ready with a good excuse. "Mama's not feeling well. And Daddy and Gram are getting ready for the picnic."

"I can't believe your mama's sick on the Fourth of July. This is practically her favorite holiday."

"It's not like she planned it, wrote on the calendar, 'Get sick on Fourth of July.'"

Ginger replaced the card she was reading. "What are you getting so riled up about?"

"Sometimes you drive me crazy, with all your rules about who you can date and when you can get sick."

"You okay, Buddy?" She studied me the way Mama did when she suspected I was coming down with a cold.

"I'm fine, or I will be if everyone will just leave me alone. I'm not a baby."

"I know that. Come on, Buddy, let's get to the firehouse before all the ice cream's gone."

"You go ahead. I have to lock up." Ginger hesitated and might have insisted on waiting for me if she hadn't spotted Jimmy Vance walking by in his tight football pants and jersey, the number eight glowing in the sunlight.

"Don't be long," she said, but I doubted she'd notice if I fell through the grate at the curb and disappeared.

As soon as Ginger was out of sight, I ran into Daddy's office at the drugstore and looked up the number for Moodus Meadows. A lady with a nasally voice answered on the fifth ring.

"I'd like to speak with Ellen Mullens, please."

"Is she a patient or on staff?"

"She's a patient. But I don't know what floor she's on." It bothered me to think of Mama as a patient. She didn't look sick.

I heard a shuffle of papers. "I'm sorry dear, but Mrs. Mullens is not receiving any calls."

"But she'll want to talk to me, I'm her daughter."

"I'm so sorry, honeybunch, but your mama doesn't have phone privileges. None of the new patients do."

"I thought Moodus Meadows was a hospital, not a prison. My mama hasn't done anything wrong. Why can't she talk to me? I have a very important message for her. It's a matter of life and death."

I heard the lady sigh and snap her gum. "Why don't you have your daddy call and speak with the doctor?"

"My daddy's busy. Besides, he doesn't know anything about what I have to tell her."

"What's your name, Hon?"

"Buddy. My name is Buddy."

"Now, sugar, why don't you give me the message and I'll write it down on one of these little pads I keep on my desk and I'll be sure to pass it on to your mama."

I thought for a minute, trying to come up with something that sounded like a life-or-death situation. "Tell her, 'Please come home.' And sign it, 'Love, Buddy.'"

"I'll get right on it and walk it over to where she's staying."

"Thank you," I said and held the phone until the connection went dead.

I finished cleaning up, erasing any evidence we'd been there and locked the door. As I slogged through the crowd to the firehouse, I imagined myself walking to the river and following its path up north. How long would it be before anyone noticed Buddy Mullens was missing?

CHAPTER EIGHT

*I*T WAS A relief to get back home after the parade. Sherry would have lingered at the firehouse all day if I'd let her. I noticed her give that fireman her number.

Questions shot from my mouth the minute I stepped through the kitchen door, feeling over-heated and grimy from the parade. "What did they say at the hospital? Did you talk to Mama?"

Fortunately, Ginger had gone home to change into her "picnic outfit," so for the time being I could stop pretending Mama was upstairs in bed, feeling a little under the weather.

Daddy worried over the brown-paper bag he was folding into a neat rectangle. "I called first thing, but Dr. Bueller didn't have much to report."

"Who's Dr. Bueller?"

"He's the staff psychiatrist. He'll be the one looking out for your mama." Daddy nodded at Gram who was stacking hot-dog buns on a tray. "I heard he's very good. Doc Gates said he knows his business."

I wrestled the bag from Daddy and laid it on the counter. "What about Mama? Did you talk to her? Does she want to come home?"

How did we know we could trust this Dr. Bueller? I wanted to talk to Mama. What if she woke up in that place and asked herself, *What am I doing here?* and then went to the head nurse and said, *Thank you very much, but I think there's been some mistake?*

Because it was a mistake to think she didn't have her wits about her. Wasn't she the one who had held us all together after Booth died, hugging everyone at the funeral, telling us everything would be all right, that there was a reason for everything, and one day we would understand why a sweet, funny, loving boy would die before he had a chance to do anything important? Like get a real job, or get married, or take his sister to the Grand Canyon.

Sure, Mama had her spells, but they were nothing new. Gram told me Mama had always been a worrier, a nervous child. Lately the spells had come closer together and lasted longer, but she'd be okay if we could get her home where she belonged.

I picked up the paper bag and rattled it in Daddy's face to get his attention. "She must have said something."

He shook his head. "Sorry, Buddy, but Dr. Bueller told me she's been real quiet since she got there. That's normal, he said."

She probably wanted to call home, and they wouldn't let her. I pictured her locked in her room, calling for help from a tiny window covered with thick metal bars.

I picked up a glass jar of mustard and slammed it against the counter. Daddy jumped inside his skin. "I want to see Mama. Now. They're treating her like a prisoner. Did you know she can't even get phone calls?"

He looked at me like I was the enemy. "Did you call the hospital?"

"I had to do something. All you can think about is getting ready for a dumb picnic. We should be with Mama. Are you going to take me to see her or not?"

"Not today, Buddy. Tomorrow. Tomorrow we'll all go over there and have a nice visit."

Gram smiled. "I'll take her some of my banana bread."

I wanted to scream and break everything in the kitchen to get their attention, to wake them up. "It's all happening again, don't you see? You're talking about banana bread. No one ever wants to talk about what's really wrong. Every time I try to talk about Booth, you're always telling me, Hush up, Buddy, you'll upset your mama. In case you haven't noticed, Booth's dead, and he left this big hole in the family that everyone keeps tiptoeing around."

Daddy went back to silently folding paper bags, concentrating so hard you would have thought his life depended on how sharp he creased the edges.

Sherry dropped the metal trough we used to ice

the pop; it clattered on the linoleum. "Listen to her. What does it take to reach you people? Buddy's speaking the truth. Whenever someone dies in this family, no one wants to talk about it."

I could have kissed Sherry a thousand times for sticking up for me.

"That's enough out of you, Sherry." Gram scowled at her youngest child and crammed more rolls onto the tray. "Buddy's upset enough without you egging her on. No good ever came of dwelling on our miseries."

"Hell's bells, Hazel! Is it dwelling to want to talk about someone you loved? After Daddy died and I wanted to talk about him, you kept telling me to be brave, to be a good girl and make him proud. And what about my brother, Tommy? He died before I was even born, and all I know about him is what I get out of Tess."

Gram squeezed a hot-dog bun until it split down the middle. "People grieve in different ways." She turned away from Sherry and looked out the window.

"It's okay, Sherry. Let Gram be," I said.

"Well, all I'm saying is, maybe if Ellen didn't

believe she had to keep everyone happy and had a chance to tell us how she was feeling, she wouldn't be spending Fourth of July in the nuthouse. That's all I'm saying." Sherry folded her arms across her chest and leaned against the refrigerator.

In the midst of our fighting, we failed to notice Tess arrive, arms laden with a chocolate cake and two apple pies. She'd changed from her costume into red pedal pushers and a blue-and-white striped T-shirt. Her short frosted brown hair needed combing. "What are you talking about? Sherry, what do you mean, Ellen's in the nuthouse? You told me she couldn't come to the parade because she had an upset stomach."

Sherry walked past Daddy and gave him a pat on his shoulder. "I'll let *you* explain what's what to Tess. Good luck." She motioned to me to help her with the trough. "Come on Buddy, best to get out of the line of fire."

Tess's voice carried all the way to the backfield. "She is royally pissed," said Sherry, as she loaded blocks of ice into the trough and I dumped in the rainbow-colored pop Daddy had ordered special. I counted ten flavors, including strawberry and lemon-lime.

"Maybe we should have stayed in there and faced the music."

"Why bother, when the music will come to us." Sherry pointed in the direction of the house and at Tess who was bearing down on us like a torpedo slipping through water. Her face turned three shades of red and her cheeks puffed in and out as she gasped for air.

"How could you not tell me about Ellen, Sherry? What are people going to think about me riding around town on a float with a ten-pound powdered wig on my head while my sister lies tormented in Moodus Meadows?"

"Nobody's going to think anything, because no one knows but us. And in case you haven't noticed, this is not about you, Tess, it's about Ellen."

"That's where you're wrong, baby sister. Everything that happens to Ellen concerns me. What right do you have to keep secrets?" Tess moved closer to Sherry until she had her pinned against a tree.

"No one's trying to keep secrets from you. We thought we'd let you enjoy your parade. Besides, there wasn't anything you could do. It happened fast, and the doctor said Ellen can't have any visitors till tomorrow."

Tess backed away and sat on one of the folding chairs placed near the picnic table. Its webbed seat sagged under her weight.

Sherry handed a bottle of cream pop to me. "Well, things can't possibly get worse. Not unless Tess here decides to make a fool of herself and complain to everybody at the picnic that we're keeping Ellen shut up against her will."

"My lips are zipped." Tess made a motion across her mouth and grabbed a lemon-lime pop from the trough. "Now, if we can just get through this picnic."

CHAPTER NINE

*G*INGER SHOWED up an hour later looking ready to pose for the cover of *Seventeen* magazine in her emerald-green shirt and matching culottes. She jumped out of her mama's car and ran toward me, her long hair lifting away from her shoulders like a yellow silk parachute.

"Is that what you're wearing?" She squinted her eyes, inspecting me from head to toe. "I thought you'd have changed by now."

"I've been helping Sherry."

Daddy passed us carrying a large bag of charcoal. "Hello, Ginger," he said. "Time to start the fires."

"Hi, Mr. Mullens. My parents said thanks for inviting them, but they had to go to some big company shindig."

Daddy nodded and ambled over to an assortment of grills set up under the oak tree in our backyard.

Gram was gone from the kitchen; her apron hung limp from the back of a chair. I spied Tess and Sherry on the front porch arguing in whispers. Sherry perched on the railing peeling away old paint. Tess stood with her back to me, but I could tell by the set of her shoulders and her clenched fists that she was beside herself with anger.

"Where is everybody? I thought this place would be crazy by now." Pepper bounded into the room and jumped on Ginger. She patted his head and pushed him down.

"It's only twelve-thirty. They'll start showing up about one." We ran up the back stairs.

"Where's your mama?"

"I told you, she doesn't feel well. She's resting."

Ginger moved away from me and walked toward my parents' bedroom. "I'll pop in and say hey to her."

"No." I grabbed her arm more roughly than I intended. "She's sleeping. And Doc Gates said she may be contagious."

Ginger rubbed the red handprint I'd left on her skin. "What do you mean she might be contagious? With what?"

I couldn't say measles or chicken pox; Ginger would know I was lying. "Strep throat. She's got it real bad. Why her throat is so red and swollen, she can't eat anything but ice cream. Doc Gates says if she coughs on anyone they'll be sicker than a dog."

"Yikes." Ginger followed me to my room. "Will she have to go to the hospital?"

"Maybe, if it turns into scarlet fever."

"And on the Fourth of July. I never heard of anyone getting scarlet fever in the summer."

"Well, it can happen, but she wants us to have the picnic anyway."

"That's so like your mama. Mine would have sent everyone home and hired a private nurse." Ginger opened my closet door, sliding the hangers back and forth, inspecting my clothes, rejecting each piece with a shake of her head.

"What are you doing?"

"Wear your new top with your white shorts." She held out the blue-and-white checked blouse, a tag hanging from the sleeve.

"I'm not wearing my new shirt. I'll wreck it serving the food." I pulled a faded pink shirt from the bottom of a pile on the floor of my closet and yanked it over my head.

"Buddy, that shirt has a stain on it." Ginger pointed to a spot in the middle of my chest.

I eyed the mark. "It's mustard. Mustard never comes out." I changed from my cutoffs to a pair of white gym shorts.

"Aren't you going to put on a different shirt?" Ginger sat in the chair by the window, her legs curled under her, thumbing through our eighth-grade yearbook.

"Why? So someone can dump potato salad on me and ruin something else? No, thank you. This is fine. Besides, one Miss America at the picnic is enough."

She picked up a dirty sock from my floor and threw it at me. "Don't make fun of me because I like to look nice."

I smiled at her. "Sorry."

"I'd give anything to have your long legs," she said. "How tall are you now? You look like you've grown."

"I try not to think about it." I inspected my legs for stubble. They needed shaving. "At the rate I'm growing, I'll have to order my clothes from one of those special Tall Girl catalogues." I kicked the cut-offs and the sock into my closet and closed the door. Secretly I hoped to get as tall and curvy as Sherry, but with my luck I'd end up tall and flat as a cardboard cutout.

"My, my, what's this?" She pointed to a photo of Jack Fletcher, the new boy in our class. He had moved to Moodus in the middle of the school year. "Why, Buddy Mullens, you drew a tiny little heart next to his picture."

"Give that back." I grabbed for the book, but she held it out of reach.

"Do you have a crush on that boy?"

I could not speak. My tongue stuck to the roof of my mouth the way it does when I eat a blob of peanut butter.

Ginger's eyes grew wide at her discovery. "So that's why you got so prissy when I said we couldn't date freshman boys." She studied Jack's photo. "We'll make an exception for Jack Fletcher. He's A-OK in my book. If he asks you out, say yes."

Who was she kidding? I'd be lucky if Jack asked me for the answers to some homework. What boy would want to go out with a girl whose mama lived in Moodus Meadows? I took the yearbook from her hands and slipped it under my bed.

"Buddy, are you all right?" Ginger's expression changed from delight to concern.

I pulled my mouth into a smile. "I'm peachy keen."

It troubled me to hide the real story about Mama from Ginger. I longed to confess the truth.

Before she had come over, I'd practiced how I'd tell her. *Here's the story, Ginger,* I'd say matter-of-factly. *My mama's real sad. She's moved into Moodus Meadows and she may never get better. So if you don't want to be friends with me anymore I'll understand.* Saying it in my head was easy; expressing the words out loud took courage I didn't have.

I'd lost Mama. I wasn't prepared to lose my friend. I feared she'd think Mama was crazy and look for signs of it in me. I wondered if craziness ran in families and if you could get it, like diabetes or poor eyesight.

"We'd better get downstairs and help out Gram."

Ginger took one last look in the mirror before she followed me to the kitchen, where the air was sticky with humidity and smelled of onions and hard-boiled eggs.

Gram and two of our neighbors, Mrs. Palmfrey and Mrs. Tremont formed an assembly line near the refrigerator; they passed bowls of salad and platters of pickles and deviled eggs to neighborhood children. One by one, they carried the plates of food to the tables set up in the field next to the barn.

Ginger made herself useful organizing games for the little kids and for a while that seemed to take her mind off Mama.

Gram joined me at the window and whispered in my ear. "I told everyone the same story. That your mama has the summer flu."

I stared at her. "I thought we agreed it was strep throat."

"It's close enough," she said and walked outside carrying the tray of rolls. I followed her with the paper napkins and more ice for the pop.

"Biggest turnout yet." Daddy waved his spatula at our neighbors, who spread out beach blankets and old bedspreads on the lawn.

Ginger gathered a bunch of kids into a circle, where they played duck-duck-goose. Then someone suggested we have a Hula Hoop contest.

"Come on, Buddy," said Ginger, as she stepped daintily into a lime-green plastic hoop and pulled it to her waist. "You can win this contest hands down."

"Nah, I don't feel like it." The last thing I wanted to do was twirl a piece of plastic around my hips for twenty minutes.

"But you beat everybody at the eighth-grade picnic." Ginger pouted her lips in my direction.

"I'm retiring from the Hula Hoop circuit. Now it's your turn to wear the crown." I ran off and busied myself helping a few of the older neighbors set up their folding chairs.

Tess assembled hamburgers and hot dogs, each one set precisely in the middle of its bun. She refused to give anyone a second helping until everyone had been served.

I had no appetite. Daddy would have told me I was lightheaded from lack of food, but I believe the mind can play tricks on you when someone you love is in trouble. Every time I turned a corner, or entered a room, I saw Mama. First it was the sight of Mrs. Miller passing out slices of apple pie that fooled my eyes into thinking Mama was home and in her rightful place at the dessert table. A few minutes later, I swore I saw the curve of her face as she bent to pick up some paper plates from the ground; it was Norma Jones, her hair the color of Mama's.

After the ice cream was finished, the kids grew impatient to light the sparklers. Mama always said the sparklers showed up better after dark, but I was just as happy that Sherry agreed to let them get an early start. The sprays of golden light would signal the end of the picnic. This year it would be a relief to be alone, to give up my pretend smile and let my face sag into sadness.

Sherry's fireman, Darren McCoy, came to call about then, still looking spiffy in his navy-blue fireman's uniform. I caught a whiff of English Leather aftershave as he passed by me in a rush to get to Sherry. He helped her organize the kids in the driveway, explaining the safest way to hold a sparkler.

We usually stayed outside long after the sun went down, playing horseshoes by candlelight. That night, the picnic broke up as soon as the last sparkler fizzled and died. Ginger wanted to sleep over, but I was too tired to keep up the charade of pretending Mama was ill in her bedroom. I sent Ginger home with the excuse of a sore throat coming on.

Sherry left with her fireman, promising to finish cleaning up in the morning. At least one person in the family seemed happy.

"Let her go," said Tess, when Gram started to protest Sherry's wiggling out of doing her share of the work. "We can handle things without her, can't we, Buddy?"

The last thing I needed was to get into the middle of an argument. I smiled at Sherry to signal her

I wasn't taking sides. "Sure, Aunt Tess. I'll put out the garbage."

I carted the trash cans down the driveway, lining them up at the curb. The thought of Aunt Tess waiting inside to give me the third degree changed my plans to go to bed early. Instead, I walked to the end of the block, beneath the tall elms. A warm breeze sweet with the scent of honeysuckle filled the night air. I paused under a giant elm, its canopy of leaves illuminated by the street lamp.

I imagined climbing its trunk, shimmying along its weathered limbs, the rough bark scratching my bare legs. I wished I could live in that tree and never come down.

CHAPTER TEN

"**W**HY CAN'T WE go now? Why do we have to wait until tonight to visit Mama?" It was the morning after the picnic, and Daddy and I sat in the kitchen eating toast made from the ends of loaves of bread. Sherry ran past us on her way out the door, late for work at JCPenney.

It gave me peace of mind to know Sherry would be back that night. "I'll stay until Ellen comes home, Buddy," she had promised me, when she returned from her date with Darren the night before. I couldn't speak to thank her over the lump in my throat. Daddy seemed reluctant to leave me alone. He offered to drop me at Gram's on his way to the drugstore, and when I insisted on staying home, he suggested I clean out the garage. An obvious ploy to keep me busy and take my mind off Mama.

"Who cares about the stupid garage? I want to make sure Mama is okay. Maybe she needs something. She didn't even take any books to read." I used my finger to write a question mark in the crumbs on my plate.

Daddy leaned against the refrigerator, still in his bathrobe. "Dr. Bueller said it would be best if we waited until this evening after dinner. They're holding some kind of get-acquainted meeting."

"You mean, Mama, you, and me? We have to talk to Dr. Bueller? Who does he think he is?"

"He's the head of Moodus Meadows, and we don't exactly have to talk to him, not alone at least. It's all the families. Sort of a get-together."

I chewed a corner of toast, but I couldn't swallow. I spit it out into my paper napkin. "All the families in one room? They expect us to spill our guts in front of strangers?"

He eyed me over the rim of his coffee mug. "It's not like that, Buddy."

"How do you know? Have you ever been to one of these things before?"

"Well, no, but I imagine Dr. Bueller will be there and other people who know what they're doing."

"How do you know that? You think just because they have a degree from some fancy school they'll be able to figure out Mama better than the people who live with her?"

He sighed and refilled his mug. "I don't want to argue with you, Buddy. Stay home if you want, we're leaving here at six-thirty."

A family meeting sounded pretty stupid to me, but it was my only chance to see Mama and to take her the new copy of *Redbook* magazine that had come in the mail. They could shove toothpicks under my fingernails; I wasn't going to talk to any of those doctors. I couldn't care less what was the matter with the rest of the people in Moodus Meadows. What did they have to do with us?

I spent a good portion of the day giving excuses

to Ginger for why I couldn't go to the pool with her, but mostly I lay in the tent on the porch making a list of ways to get Mama out of Moodus Meadows.

I was up to number seven—*Infest the place with fleas collected from Pepper*—when Daddy arrived home with Gram in tow. He ate leftover macaroni salad while standing in front of the open refrigerator door and told me to get a move on if I wanted to go see Mama.

Gram rode up front, dressed in her blue silk dress and straw hat with the lilies of the valley on the brim. You'd think she was going to church instead of to a place where people wore jackets with arms that tied across their chests. At the last minute Sherry came peeling down the driveway screaming for us to wait, she wanted to go with us. She didn't even know where we were headed; she could never bear to be left behind.

"I'm family," she said, when Daddy suggested she might be bored. "What kind of a person do you think I am?" Sherry climbed into the backseat next to me. "Is Tess coming?"

Gram turned and the lilies of the valley bobbed on their stems. "Tess is meeting us there. She's bringing some things for Ellen."

Tess waited for us in her car in the Moodus Meadows parking lot.

"I'll bet Ellen will be real happy to see us," she said, as she wrestled a large-leafed plant and a blue-and-green area rug from the back of her car.

Sherry almost bust a gut laughing. "What comes next Tess, draperies and major appliances? Ellen's here because she's lost her marbles and you're acting like she's moving into her college dorm."

Tess dropped the plant, barely missing Sherry's foot. "You always have to spoil everything, Sherry. You're just upset because you didn't think to bring something for Ellen."

Sherry lit a cigarette and dropped the match into the plant. "What am I spoiling? Has everyone forgotten why we're here? This is not a birthday party, in case you haven't noticed."

Daddy picked up the plant and placed it between our two cars. "Let's leave this here for now." He smiled at Tess. "It was thoughtful of you."

Tess clamped the rug under her arm. "Well, I'm taking her the rug. These places always have those cold linoleum floors. Nothing worse when you step out of bed in the morning."

Sherry rolled her eyes. "I can think of a few worse things, like waking up in this place for starters."

"Girls, stop bickering. People are staring." Gram pushed past us and headed for the sign that said MAPLE COTTAGE, Mama's temporary home.

A woman wearing a red Hawaiian print shirt and white pedal pushers ushered us into a windowed sun porch. The air smelled stale, like an attic filled with old clothes. We found Mama sitting on a window seat gazing through the glass at a bird feeder. Tess was wrong about her being happy to see us. She didn't even turn when I touched her on the shoulder and said, "Mama, I'm here."

"Ellen's not being cooperative," said a tall, skinny man wearing green plaid pants and a short-sleeved white shirt, as he passed out blank name tags and pens to family members trickling into the room. Most of them looked scared.

Sherry printed MARILYN MONROE on her name tag and stuck it over her right breast. Tess ripped the tag off Sherry and stuffed it into the pocket of her shorts. She sighed, unrolled the rug and lowered herself next to Mama. "Lord save me," she said in a whisper.

We sat on the window seat, scrunched around Mama, with me holding her hand. At least she didn't pull away. Dr. Bueller came into the room and introduced himself. A tall man with thinning brown hair, he wore a light blue short-sleeved shirt buttoned to the collar, gray trousers baggy at the knees and scuffed brown loafers. He gave a speech about how we were all there to help each other, one big happy family and all that, and we should feel free to talk about what was on our minds.

"There are no secrets in this room," he said before he sat in a wicker chair.

"Good," said Sherry. "Now we'll finally learn Tess's weight."

"Hush up, Sherry. Do you always have to be the

center of attention?" Tess popped a hard candy into her mouth and offered one to me.

"No thanks, Aunt Tess," I said and pointed to the punch and cookies set out on TV trays. "I'll have some of that if I get hungry."

"Who'd like to begin?" Dr. Bueller nodded at a young woman perched on a footstool. She had stringy brown hair and wore weathered jeans and a white knit top.

"Hi, my name is Patti with an *i*, and this is my mom." She pointed to a tired-looking woman sitting behind her, neatly dressed in a black linen sheath and pearls.

"I've been at Moodus Meadows since April. My mother was worried about me because I didn't want to go out with my friends. What's wrong with wanting to spend time in my room? I wasn't hurting anyone. It's okay here, I guess. They let me read and if I make up the work I can graduate with my high-school class next year."

A man sitting across from me stood and gave a little wave to everyone. "Mostly, I'm plain tired. Before I came here, I slept fourteen hours a day. Got up, went to work, came home and climbed back into bed. Oh, my name's Henry."

Henry looked about thirty. He wore jeans, a plaid shirt, and work boots. "Doc Bueller says I isolate myself."

He pulled at his brown wavy hair, which touched the collar of his shirt. "Every day I'm supposed to talk to three people for at least five minutes." Henry turned to Dr. Bueller. "Does this count as one of the times?"

"Yes, it does, Henry. For some of the new people here, this may seem strange, but our goal is to make you comfortable enough to join in on family nights."

It didn't take long before most of the other patients told their stories of what landed them at Moodus Meadows. A few relatives shared their feelings, but mostly they avoided eye contact with anyone in the room.

Sherry spent the "sharing time" chiseling at a painted-shut window sash with a metal nail file in a vain attempt to open it and get us some fresh air. Daddy looked about to die from the heat, his face pink and sweaty as a canned ham. Gram kept herself busy hand-piecing quilt squares she carried in a canvas bag.

Every minute or two Tess tried to engage Mama with a smile or a pat on her knee. Mama refused to turn from the bird feeder, preferring squawking blue jays to the babblers in the room. I was disappointed she wasn't happier to see me, but what did I expect from a woman turned inside out?

After anyone who wanted to had had their say, and the punch bowl was drained, the place cleared out about as fast as a building on the last day of school. We remained with Mama, grateful for some privacy.

"Look, Ellen, I bought you a nice rug, something warm to put your feet on in the morning. Aren't the colors pretty, all blue and green?" Tess pointed to the stripes one at a time, as if Mama didn't know the difference between blue and green.

"I want to go back to my room." It was the first thing out of Mama's mouth since we got there. Not a bright beginning.

"This is family night, Ellen," said a woman who introduced herself as Mama's nurse. She wore a yellow-and-white striped shirtwaist dress with a skirt big enough to house the circus and large white earrings in the shape of daisies. She must have spent an hour teasing and spraying her red hair into the shape of a football helmet. The name tag on her chest read VERONICA BIXBY, RN.

She leaned over Mama like a cloud shutting out the sun. "Ellen, don't you want to talk to your family? They have to leave in a few minutes."

Mama ignored her suggestion. Nurse Bixby reminded me of a Brownie leader I once had who pretended to be your friend so she could pump you for information.

"Why don't we take a walk outside." Daddy pulled Mama to her feet. I knew this was hard on him. He valued privacy above all wealth.

Nurse Bixby piped up, "Oh, Ellen doesn't have outside privileges."

"What are you talking about?" Daddy's face flushed even redder.

"Why don't the two of us chat in the kitchen?" Old Bixby cast a suspicious glance at me and took hold of Daddy's elbow.

"You can talk in front of my daughter. Buddy knows what's what."

I loved him for sticking up for me. "Why can't she go outside?" No wonder Mama spent her time looking out at the birds and trees. She was starving for oxygen.

"We have rules. At Moodus Meadows everyone must follow a strict schedule if they want to get better. Doctor feels the first week should be one of introspection and observation. Then when we get to know Ellen better she may begin some other activities."

Tess finished rolling up the rug. "What the hell is she talking about?"

Sherry grabbed a cookie someone had missed. "I think she means Ellen needs to think about what got her here in the first place and then figure out how she's gonna get out."

Nurse Bixby laughed high and squeaky like a cartoon mouse. "Not quite," she said. "Ellen needs to come to terms with why she's not feeling herself. She'll also have time to talk to other residents and make some friends."

"My brother died," I said.

"Oh, I'm sorry to hear that," said Nurse Bixby, but she didn't look at me, so I doubted her sincerity.

"That's why Mama's here. Because my brother died." I said it louder this time. Mama put out her hand to stop me from saying more, as if my saying it in public made Booth's death more real.

"His name was Booth. He was a good brother; he never treated me like a baby. But he's dead." I turned toward Mama. "He's been dead for two years, Mama. I know how much you're hurting, but we all are. Daddy, Gram, Tess, and Sherry. We miss him like crazy, but now we don't even have you."

Mama covered her ears with her hands, but I knew she heard me. Tears streamed from her eyes and dribbled from her chin. Part of me wanted to blot her face with a tissue, real tender-like, but the evil Buddy, the girl tired of keeping her feelings bottled up for fear I'd upset Mama, was blissful at causing a commotion. Maybe it was cruel to make Mama cry, but at least I'd cracked her shell and got a reaction. Any response was better than talking to a zombie.

"Say something, Mama," I yelled at her, my own face close enough to hers to feel her breath.

"Don't, Buddy, let your mama have a rest here." Daddy took hold of my hand, but I pulled away and ran outside.

The parking lot lay in darkness, and I tripped over Tess's plant as I ran between the cars. I yanked at its green spikes until the root ball pulled free from the pot, then I pitched it overhand and sent it spinning in an arc over the roof of Daddy's Buick. It came down like a bomb and smashed on the pavement.

Tess didn't say anything about the plant. She gave me a hug good-bye, helped Gram into her car, and tossed the blue-and-green rug on the backseat. I felt sorry for her.

During the ride home, Daddy listened to the ball game on the radio. Sherry chain-smoked, tossing the cigarette butts out the window. They scattered on the pavement, sparkling in the dark.

When we got home, I waited for the other shoe to drop, for Daddy to sit me down and tell me he was disappointed in me. Instead, he kissed me good night, and told me to sleep late in the morning. Sherry let me have the bottom bunk, saying that maybe I'd sleep better in my own bed. She could have slept in the guest room, but I was relieved when she climbed the ladder to the top bunk and settled herself above me like a guardian angel.

It came as unexpected, the way they forgave me for my outburst at Moodus Meadows, as if I had knocked a vase off the mantel, expecting it to break into a million pieces, and instead it had landed intact. I wondered if they were letting sleeping dogs lie, or if they feared I was as crazy as Mama.

We slept with the windows open wide. Sometime during the night I woke to the sound of thunder. The sky came alive with bolts of lightning so fierce they lit up my room and turned night into day. "It's only the angels clearing away the dust," I whispered to myself.

CHAPTER ELEVEN

*T*HE NEXT morning Daddy came into my room at dawn and woke Sherry. I pretended to be asleep and heard them whispering about Daddy having to go down to the store to fill a prescription for someone with bronchitis. Sherry told him she'd hold down the fort. She didn't have to go into work until noon.

By eight o'clock I had to pee real bad, but I waited until Sherry went downstairs before I tiptoed to the bathroom. I didn't want to talk about what had happened the night before.

I dressed in shorts and a T-shirt and managed to

sneak down the back stairs. Sherry was drinking coffee and smoking a cigarette on the front porch. I grabbed a piece of coffee cake left on the kitchen table before I ran to the barn for my bike. She'd find my note taped to the refrigerator when she came inside.

GONE TO SEE VERNA, I wrote on a paper napkin. Pepper almost gave me away with his whining, but I quieted him with the last of my crumbcake.

I rode my bike through town and out to River Road. The storm of the night before had done little to relieve the humidity. The sky to the east darkened as I peddled faster; cumulus clouds chased after me like waves that could pound me down.

The route I took cut through a forest of tall pines, opened onto fallow fields that curved along the river, and ended at a clearing where my friend Verna Kaye Sanford lived with her family in a ramshackle house. The cottage, with its tin roof and sagging porch, overlooked the town garbage heap; most people in Moodus referred to it as "the dump house."

The dump house had once belonged to some

summer people named Boswell. Mama told me they had a fit when the dump was relocated a stone's throw from their front door. Rather than pay their taxes, they abandoned the place. Mama told me the Boswells' loss was the Sanfords' gain.

No one knew where the Sanfords came from; one day they appeared like a band of Gypsies and settled into the dump house. Parker Sanford, Verna's daddy, elected himself keeper of the dump and in return for his services, they got to live there rent free.

Keeping the dump was his part-time job; his main business was raising birds for cockfighting. Cockfighting was illegal, but as long as he took his business out of the county, no one bothered him. He was a scary man, small and wiry with coarse dark hair and wild eyebrows set above eyes so black they appeared to have no pupils. His smoking made him prone to fits of coughing. I kept my distance.

Usually I met up with Verna on neutral ground, but that day I made an exception because I needed to see her real bad. She never did show up at the parade or the picnic. Since they had no phone I couldn't call to check on her, to make sure she wasn't mad at me.

The Sanford kids were already outside, making a racket rolling each other down the hill in metal garbage cans. I spotted Tammy's red curls as she spun out of control and crashed into a tree.

"I'm okay, Verna," she yelled as she crawled from the garbage can and dusted herself off. She was still in her pajamas, rolled up to her knees and covered with dirt.

"Hey, Buddy," eleven-year-old Russell called to me. Verna snatched him to her and told him to get back in the house and put on some shoes. He was small for his age, with a pointed head covered by dark hair that always looked uncombed because of the cowlicks that scrambled it in all directions. The boys at school called him "Pinhead" and worse if Verna wasn't around to protect him.

It took Russell two years to get out of first grade. His teachers gave up on him as a lost cause and each year passed him on to the next grade. He could barely read the baby books Verna got him out of the library.

"Hey, Buddy, I thought you fell off the face of the earth. Where you been?" Verna stood next to the mailbox, wearing a red-checked dress with giant rickrack, probably someone's curtains in another life. Ever since a do-gooder had deposited an old Singer sewing machine with a note taped to it saying *It works* on the Sanfords' porch, Verna had been sewing her own clothes.

"I've been busy with all the chores Daddy keeps thinking up for me to do. We missed you at the picnic."

"I had to take care of Mama and the babies."

"I'm not a baby," shouted Russell as he ran by and grabbed one of Verna's pigtails. She wore her light-brown hair parted in the middle, held back with rubber bands, tight enough to almost pull her eyes around the sides of her head. Most days she got worn thin with work, but her lips naturally turned up at the corners, so she always appeared to be smiling.

"Shoot, Russell, I wasn't talking about you. Keep your hands to yourself before I take a switch to you."

Russell danced out of Verna's reach, sticking his tongue out at both of us. "Can't catch me, can't catch me!" He was bare-chested and wore a pair of cutoff men's trousers pulled tight with a rope belt.

There were seven Sanford children in all. Verna was born smack in the middle, and ever since the older kids had moved away, she'd gotten stuck with the three youngest—eleven-year-old Russell, seven-year-old Tammy, and her baby sister, Jane, who would turn two on Halloween. They mostly ran wild in the summertime, eating whatever they found on the shelves, taking baths in the creek that ran behind the property, and hiding from Verna when she called them in at bedtime. On days when I felt the weight of the world on my shoulders, I looked at Verna and counted my blessings.

Verna motioned for me to follow her. "Let's sit in the tent for a while. It's the only place I get a minute's peace."

The green canvas tent, another cast-off rescued from the dump, sat in the middle of a circle of forsythia bushes. Verna forbade her brother or sisters to enter, threatening them with unseen horrors, like worms in their beds or liver for breakfast, if they disobeyed.

The inside of the tent smelled musty from the previous night's rain. A sleeping bag lay open on an old piece of oilcloth. Two cookie tins decorated with Christmas scenes wedged a dozen books on a makeshift shelf made of cinder blocks and a plank of wood.

"I got candy. Want some?" Verna opened one of the tins, passed me a square of chocolate, and took one for herself. We leaned back on some pillows piled in the corner and sucked on the candy.

"How's your mama?" I asked to be polite. Rina's condition never changed. She'd been mostly bedridden since she caught polio when Verna was five years old. The people at the hospital gave her some metal braces to wear on her legs, but according to Verna, she hated them, said they made her lurch like a monster.

"I got her out on the porch yesterday. Put on her leg braces for her and fixed a place for her to rest." Verna pulled back the canvas flap and pointed to an orange crate padded with cushions.

"Did she like being outside?"

Verna sighed. "She lasted ten minutes until somebody came by asking after my daddy. 'Get me inside, Verna,' she says to me like she's scared to let them see her. Look, see how she bruised my shinbone banging into me with her braces." I saw a faint blue smudge on Verna's leg. "She didn't mean to hurt me, can't help herself when she gets scared."

It occurred to me that our mamas had a lot in common. Verna's mama, Rina, feared the world because she looked different on the outside; my mama hid away in Moodus Meadows because she felt different on the inside.

I ached to confide in Verna, to relate the tale of how Mama lost her mind. How do you stay so strong and brave? I would ask her. Mostly I yearned to know if she ever hated Rina for not being like everyone else's mama. For not being normal.

Verna handed me a cherry sucker from the pocket of her dress. "It was Russell's, but he doesn't need it, his teeth are rotten."

"Want to come to the library with me? I promised Miss De LaTour I'd help her dust and shelve the books. She's expecting a new shipment, and we can have first dibs."

"I can't." Verna looked toward the house. "Got to get Mama's lunch and give her a bath."

I wondered which was worse, having your mama home, lying in a bed, or off in Moodus Meadows, living among strangers.

Verna traced the rickrack on her skirt with her index finger. "How was the picnic?"

"You didn't miss anything. Except for Timmy setting Nancy's hair on fire with a sparkler, it was dull as vanilla ice cream." I watched Russell turn his back to us and pee against a tree.

"Russell, don't you be doing that. We've got company."

Russell closed up his pants and smiled at me. "Buddy's not company." He came toward the tent, stopping at the opening. "Can I have some chocolate, Verna?"

"You'll spoil your lunch. I've got a pot of beans in the oven."

"We got hot dogs?"

Verna shooed him away from the tent. "No, but

we got brown bread and butter. Now, go find your shoes before you step on a nail."

He ran off in search of his shoes. Verna followed him up the slope to their house, motioning me to follow her.

"I've got to go," I said.

"Come by again this afternoon."

"I'll try, but it might have to wait until tomorrow."

"You could stay over. We can sleep in the tent and read by flashlight."

"I said I'll try."

"Promise?" She gazed toward the dumpkeeper's shack. "My daddy's not here. He's gone over to Kerryville for the cockfights. Packed up his birds and left before dawn. He won't get home till tomorrow."

I didn't have the heart to tell her it gave me the creeps to hang around that place. Even with her daddy gone, it got spooky there at night.

"So, will you sleep over?" Verna nudged me.

Maybe if her daddy were away it wouldn't be so bad. Even if I didn't have the nerve to confide in her about Mama, it calmed me being near her. "I'll see, okay?"

"But you'll stop by on your way home no matter what?" She tugged at the plastic fringe hanging from the handlebars on my bike.

"I said so, didn't I? Now I have to get going. See you later, alligator."

Verna backed away and smiled at me. "After a while, crocodile."

CHAPTER TWELVE

*T*HE MONTH of July evaporated faster than raindrops on a hot sidewalk. I've heard the saying that time flies when you're having fun; it also moves too quickly when you are working against a deadline. In spite of Ginger taking charge of my social life, I did my best to make plans to get Mama out of Moodus Meadows before the start of school.

Daddy, Sherry, Tess, Gram, and I attended those family meetings at Moodus Meadows every week. They never got easier. Sherry said the get-togethers reminded her of every bad blind date she'd been on. But they were even worse, she said, because instead of being forced to make small talk with one weird stranger, you had to do it with dozens.

Mama did make more of an effort to act as if she were glad to see us. I never did get past the feeling that I was a visitor and didn't belong. When I visited Mama, I felt out of place. Sometimes I caught my-self grabbing hold of a wall or a piece of furniture to keep my balance. I felt jealous when I saw her making friends with the other patients; she should have been spending the summer with me.

I usually looked forward to the end of August, to the hot steamy days that gave you the excuse to sit in the pond, up to your neck in cool water, or to lie limp in the hammock sheltered by the twin maples. Mama and I would circle a date on the calendar with a big red loop; mark it as a day to shop for school supplies and a new outfit for me to start school.

Things were different the summer of Mama's episode. August came and brought the bad news that mama might not be out of Moodus Meadows by the start of school. Dr. Bueller told us Mama was making progress; she talked more about her sadness. The danger seemed past, but I knew it could flare up at any time.

Sherry, Daddy, and I got into a rhythm of waking up, doing what we needed to do during the day and coming together at night. Within our misshapen family, pulled out of kilter with Mama gone, the three of us went through the motions as if everything were normal.

The story we decided to tell anyone who asked was that Mama recovered from her strep throat and had gone off to Atlanta to help out a distant cousin with her new baby. Sherry later amended the story to say the cousin had twins. She said it sounded more urgent.

Most days, Ginger dragged me to the town pool. We lounged on giant towels, our bodies slathered with Coppertone suntan lotion. Ginger wore a new cherry-red Jantzen bathing suit. Mama and I never did go shopping for a new suit, so I got stuck wearing last year's model with its faded pink flowers and saggy-baggy seat. Ginger spent as much time at the snack bar as she did in the water. A handsome boy named Brad Vickers gave her free slushies and told her she had the best tan at the pool.

I practiced my backstroke and walking on my hands underwater in the shallow end. Little kids cannonballing off the edge of the pool almost killed me; their mamas sat in folding chairs they brought from home, gossiping with each other and drinking iced tea from Dixie cups.

Mostly I read paperback mysteries behind dark glasses, casting glances around the pool every so often in hopes of seeing Jack Fletcher. Not that I would have done a simple thing to attract his attention if I did see him, but I looked anyway.

I got up the courage to stay over at Verna's, making sure her daddy was off with his birds at the cockfights in Kerryville. We played Scrabble by flashlight in the tent. Some nights Verna allowed Russell inside, putting him in charge of the tiles. He took his job seriously, as if it might be something he would do for the rest of his life.

Missed opportunities came and went, and I never did tell Ginger or Verna the truth about Mama. What would be worse, them finding out from me or from someone else? I bit my tongue and took my chances.

Once when I suggested to Daddy it might be okay to tell our friends about Mama, he shook his head in dismay as if I wanted to trade secrets with the enemy.

"Think of your Mama's job, Buddy. She needs to have something waiting for her, something to give her purpose. People get strange ideas when they hear someone is shaky in the head. Do you think those parents will want their children getting guidance from a woman who's been in Moodus Meadows?"

"Mama's not crazy."

"You and I know that, but people can turn on you. Sometimes the people you least expect. I learned that when Booth died. There were friends who suddenly got busy every time I called to say hey. Death scares people; they don't want to stand too close. The same goes for illness, especially one you can't see, like the sickness that's got hold of your mama."

"If you ask me, it's a witch trial." Sherry checked

out her makeup in the kitchen mirror. "That's what I hate about small towns. Be a little different and you're called weird. If Ellen lived in New York City, she could walk around Times Square with a paper bag over her head and bowling shoes on her feet and no one would bat an eyelash."

"So you're saying Daddy's right, and we shouldn't tell anyone the truth about Mama?"

Sherry shook her head. "Not if she wants to be able to shop in Winn-Dixie without people clutching their children when she passes." Sherry dropped her lipstick into her purse and snapped the latch. "One of these days when I have a little money I'm getting out of Moodus."

Since getting out of Moodus wasn't an option for me, I'd have to come up with a plan to bring Mama home. Her recuperation moved along slower than an ant through syrup. Dr. Bueller reported to Daddy that Mama couldn't be rushed. He said it had taken years for her to get to the end of her rope; it might take months for her to recover.

I didn't have months to spare, two weeks at best. I needed to get Mama out of that place before school started. Surely Daddy could not lie to Mr. Peebles, the principal, and tell him Mama was staying with a sick friend. A self-righteous man, he'd snoop until he figured out the whole sorry story.

The responsibility to bring Mama home landed squarely on my shoulders. On a hot Monday morning in August, soon after Daddy and Sherry left for work, I got ready to put my scheme into action. Number one on my list was to make contact with Mama so she didn't forget us, shut away in that place.

Except for the weekly family meetings, we barely got to see her. Dr. Bueller said the separation was part of her therapy, to wean Mama from her family. He said if we could reassure her that we could survive without her, she might believe she wasn't responsible for Booth's death.

I could have told her that at home. What if Mama decided we didn't need her anymore? Dr. Bueller might have a fancy degree, but he didn't know everything. I needed to see Mama alone, face-to-face, with no Nurse Bixby butting into our conversation.

If I called ahead, it would eliminate the element of surprise I needed to avoid a roadblock. I'd seen the way Dr. Bueller analyzed every word we said in those family meetings. He probably told Mama she'd feel better if she spilled her guts about her awful family.

No one could keep me away from Mama. I fed Pepper his kibble, then hopped on my bike and took Sherman Avenue to Moodus Meadows. The more I imagined Dr. Bueller putting ideas in Mama's head, the faster I pedaled my bicycle. Wearing a pink voile Sunday dress with stockings and white leather flats to make me look older, I got sweaty as a pig on a spit. The net crinoline designed to make the skirt of my dress stand out wider than an open umbrella scratched my legs raw.

Arriving at Moodus Meadows, I tried to sneak in the front door to Maple Cottage, but it was locked. I backtracked to the main entrance, hid my bike behind some overgrown azaleas and walked to the front door. As I stepped into the foyer I heard classical music, accompanied by the clatter of a typewriter.

The lady at the front desk, identified as June Small by a brass plaque placed next to a vase of daisies, looked up from her typing and smiled. "How may I help you?"

"I'm here to see Ellen Mullens. She's expecting me."

"Just a moment, dear." Miss Small spun her chair away from me and pressed a button on her phone.

She whispered a few words into the mouthpiece, and listened to someone on the other end. Probably Nurse Bixby ordering Miss Small to call security and have me escorted from the grounds.

I wouldn't leave without a fight. I'd plant my caboose on the floor and refuse to budge. They'd have to drag me against my will, the way the police did to those brave colored people who fought for their right to sit at the lunch counter at Woolworth's Five and Dime. If they could be strong enough to demand to be treated equal, to eat at the Woolworth's counter same as white people, then I would tie myself to Miss Small's desk if necessary, to see Mama.

Prepared for the worst, I looked around for

something to grab on to, a bit of rope or twine to tie around my wrist, to anchor me to the leg of the desk.

Miss Small hung up the phone and drew me a little map. "Go through these doors, dear, and follow the signs that say 'Maple Cottage.'"

"Thank you." I smiled at her, feeling ashamed that only moments before I imagined beaning her with her stapler if she gave me any trouble. "Thanks for the map."

"You're very welcome. That's a lovely dress you're wearing."

"Thank you." I didn't need the map, but I took it anyway, not wanting to hurt her feelings. Too bad I hadn't thought to bring a change of clothes, so I could get out of my dress.

I walked through a passageway that connected the main building to a tree-shaded courtyard. The back door to Maple Cottage stood open. Two ladies rolling piecrusts at the kitchen counter smiled at me as I passed.

A young man with an uneven crew cut lounged on the couch in the living room, his long legs draped over the armrest. He looked up from the fly-fishing magazine he'd been reading and stared at me.

"I'm looking for Ellen Mullens."

He hesitated, pursing his lips in and out like a fish. "Oh, Ellen. She's probably in the back garden trying to save a tree."

"I don't think she has outside privileges."

"What's your name?" He looked me over again as if he might have missed something important the first time.

"Buddy, Buddy Mullens."

"You must be Ellen's kid." He sat up and tossed his magazine onto a pile of newspapers on the floor. "You kind of look like her in a serious, the-world-is-too-much-for-me way."

I came close to telling him from where I stood it looked like he was the one who couldn't handle the world, but I needed information. "So, where do you think she is?"

"I'm telling you, she's outside. She did whatever old Bixby wanted her to do and she got promoted."

"Thanks." The worst had happened. They had managed to brainwash Mama. "See you later."

"Not if I can help it." He flopped on the couch and turned his face to the cushions, pulling an afghan over his head.

I wondered where everyone could be, especially Nurse Bixby. The thought of her lurking somewhere left me uneasy. At any moment she might step from behind a curtain and scream, "Child on the grounds. Off with her head." Sort of like that nasty queen in *Alice in Wonderland*.

A glass passageway led toward the bedrooms, the better to keep an eye on the patients. I tiptoed along the threadbare carpet, watching my feet, which I hardly recognized in their girlie shoes. I stopped to fix my nylons, bagging at the ankles; a motion from outside caught my attention. Several people I remembered from family night hopped about, performing some kind of weird group dance. They swayed their arms like tree branches blowing in the wind. Their loose summer clothes billowed, taut sails above a sea of grass.

Let me guess, I said to myself. Who would be the ringleader of this motley crew? The musical-comedy scene had Mama's name on it. Letting myself out through a French door, I stepped around a record player set on a TV tray. Its extension cord ran across the walkway to an open window. Doris Day singing *"Que Será Será"* blasted from the speakers. "Whatever will be, will be." How many times had Mama and I sung that song in the car? She called it our theme song.

Reluctant to interrupt their dance, I sat beneath a tree, careful to tuck my legs underneath my dress so I wouldn't get it grass stained.

The lawn dancers weren't bad. The music ended and they slowed their steps and clapped. "Better than ever," announced a voice I recognized as Mama's.

The group parted; Mama strode across the lawn to put on a new record, this one Patti Page singing "How Much Is That Doggie in the Window?" On her way back to join the group Mama noticed me, and without missing a beat, extended her hand.

"Come dance with us, Buddy." She wore a white cotton dress with half a dozen pastel-colored chiffon scarves tied to her belt. The scarves flew about, turning her into a pinwheel as she ran across the lawn with me in tow.

Eager to be with Mama, to touch her, I would have danced over hot coals. I joined hands with her and sang the words to "How Much Is That Doggie in the Window?" while Mama's dance troupe cavorted around us barking like puppies.

Maybe we were all crazy, lost souls bumping into each other to music. But on that hot summer day, with my toes pinched into tight knots by my too-small shoes, I heard my off-key voice blend with Mama's pure alto, and for a small space of time I forgot to be afraid.

CHAPTER THIRTEEN

"**W**HY ARE YOU wearing that getup?" Sherry asked as soon as I walked through the kitchen door. She stood at the stove frying up hamburgers.

"I went to see Mama. I was afraid they wouldn't let me in unless I looked older."

Sherry laughed as she flipped the burgers. "Buddy, you look like a giant peony in that dress."

"We can't all be fashion plates." I pressed the skirt down and it sprung back like a pop-up doll. "Tess bought it for me last Easter."

"It looks like something she'd pick out." She put down the spatula and gave me a hug. "I'm sorry for teasing, but I've never seen you put on a dress without a struggle."

"Who cares? It got me into Moodus Meadows."

"You didn't mention anything about going there this morning."

"If I had, would you have told me not to go?"

"Probably. I don't want to see you get hurt. I see how sad you get every time we visit her."

"It was different today."

Sherry came over to the table and sat down. "How'd it go?"

"Good, real good."

"Did I hear you say you went to see your mama?" Daddy stood in the doorway obviously eavesdropping on our conversation. He sat down at the table and told me to go on with my story.

"She's putting on a show. Like Judy Garland and Mickey Rooney did in those movies. Mama's got everyone organized into singers and dancers. Anyone who can't perform has to make scenery or do posters. Except for a boy named Robbie, I met him today. He's kind of rude, and Mama says he stays mostly to himself. But she's working on him, says he'll come around when he sees how much fun they're having."

"Leave it to Ellen to find a cause, even in that place. She loves to rescue people." Sherry put a bottle of ketchup on the table.

"It's not like that, Sherry. I met all the people in her cottage and they're okay. There's a minister named Bill, who preached a sermon when he was drunk, so his congregation thought he needed a rest. And a woman named Myra who used to be a prima ballerina until she got bad ankles and had to retire and then one day she realized she had nothing to get out of bed for, so she didn't. She didn't get out of bed for a month, until her sister made a fuss and took her to Moodus Meadows. Oh, and a man named Alfred who had a little stroke and got depressed. He can't talk too well, but he does fine if he sings the words. So he sings all the time, like someone in an opera."

"Sounds like quite a crew." Sherry passed around the burgers and took a seat.

Daddy shook his finger to caution me. "Don't get too attached to those people, Buddy. They may seem all right, but they're in Moodus Meadows for a reason."

I took the bowl of french fries from Sherry and placed it in the middle of the table. "They're sad Daddy, that's how they ended up at Moodus Meadows. But they wouldn't hurt me."

Daddy squirted a blob of ketchup on his burger. "I didn't mean to imply any of those people would hurt you, Buddy, but Moodus Meadows is not a place for children. You let your Mama get better and she'll be home before you know it. The doctors and nurses know what they're doing."

It was impossible to reason with him. "I'm going back on Saturday. Mama said she could use some help with the costumes."

Daddy took a spoonful of baked beans. "I don't think that's such a good idea, you spending so much time there. The other patients might not like it. You need to respect their privacy."

"They like me, Daddy. They made me promise to come back."

Sherry put up her hand for attention. "What about Nurse Bixby? You think she's going to like you invading her territory?"

"I didn't even see her today."

154

Daddy stopped eating and put down his fork. "I'll give Dr. Bueller a call and see what he thinks."

I dropped my burger on my plate and stood up. "No, do not call him. It's okay. I want to be there with Mama."

Daddy looked to Sherry for help. "I'll go with Buddy on Saturday," said Sherry. "I don't have to work."

I knew Sherry meant well, but for once I wanted to solve my own problems. "Thanks, but I told Mama I'd come alone. We have a deal. I can come as long as I don't ask her if she's getting better or say anything about home."

Sherry stacked our dirty plates and carried them to the sink. "Well, a deal's a deal. But call me if you need a ride or anything."

"I'll be fine. Don't call Dr. Bueller. Promise me, Daddy?"

He took a drink of milk; a white mustache outlined his upper lip. "All right, Buddy. But I don't want you disappointed if your mama changes her mind."

"She won't." I'd make sure of that.

CHAPTER FOURTEEN

*T*HE NEXT week I made two trips to visit Mama, each time managing to avoid Nurse Bixby. Mama told me her acting troupe had decided to put on an abbreviated version of the musical *Oklahoma!* A lady named Nelda knew all the songs by heart and played them on an old upright piano.

"A musical is nothing without costumes," Mama said to the players when they assembled after lunch. "The men can wear their own pants with nice shirts and bandannas. Davis is in charge of finding some cowboy hats and boots."

She turned to me. "We need gingham, Buddy,

and fringe for the skirts." Mama paced back and forth on the stage of Harvest House, a cottage used for meetings and programs.

"Yes, and the ladies should wear sunbonnets with satin ribbons."

"Maybe you could find some things at the Trade-A-Way. Ask your daddy for five dollars."

"I don't think they're going to have sunbonnets and old-fashioned dresses."

Her brow creased with concern. "I want this to be special. There's no sense putting on a show if we're going to look like fools."

The others agreed, and came up with the bright idea of sewing their own outfits. Unfortunately, they didn't have a piece of fabric or a spool of thread among them. And except for Mama, who could sew on a button in a pinch, none of them could sew a stitch.

"I've got an idea. Let me work on it. Don't worry about the costumes. Just practice your singing and dancing." I kissed Mama good-bye, got my bike from where I had stashed it behind Maple Cottage, and took off for home.

In the excitement of being with Mama, I had

completely forgotten I was supposed to do something with Ginger and I was running late.

"Ginger's upstairs," Sherry announced as I ran into the kitchen, feeling more hopeful than I had in weeks. Even Ginger's wrath could not spoil my joy from spending the afternoon with Mama. "She showed up an hour ago."

"I completely forgot. Did you tell her where I was?"

Sherry made a face at me, crossing her eyes and sticking out her tongue. "Do I look like an idiot? What you tell your friends about Ellen is your business."

Sherry gave me the once over as she poked a pot roast simmering in the oven. Lately, she'd been cooking fancy meals, which was any meal with more than one vegetable.

"You know, sometimes it feels better if you have someone to talk to besides family. Maybe you should trust Ginger. I don't think she'd tell anyone else."

"Are these for dinner?" I pointed to a basket of corn muffins. I couldn't tell Sherry the real reason I didn't confide in Ginger was because I thought she'd be afraid to be my friend.

Sherry held out the basket. "Gram sent them over with Tess, who by the way said she'd take you by to visit Ellen tonight if you're interested."

I bit off a piece of muffin. "Did you tell her I went to see Mama by myself?"

"No, I figured it was none of her business."

"Why don't you go with her? Mama would love to see you."

Sherry got a big grin on her face. "I'm going out tonight. Darren's coming here for dinner and then he's taking me dancing."

"Maybe he's in love." I grabbed another muffin and climbed the back stairs.

Ginger perched on the chair near the window holding stands of her hair up to the light, searching for split ends.

"Well, it's about time, Buddy. What happened to you? I've been waiting for over an hour."

"Sorry, I forgot." I tossed her the muffin, then flopped onto the bottom bunk. The bed springs creaked under my weight.

"You forget everything lately." She said this in a soft voice so I knew she'd already moved past anger to forgiveness. "I'm thinking of putting a red rinse in my hair. You can buy those little capsules with the dye inside at the five and dime."

I studied her for a moment and tried to imagine red hair against her pale skin. "I think you'd look good. Especially with your blue eyes."

"Okay, that problem is solved. Now, what are we going to do with you?" She leaped up and rushed toward me, a human hurricane. She grabbed my hands and yanked me from the bed.

I sighed and rolled my eyes. "I'm fine." I fingered my own hair. Mama used to cut it for me, and it was long overdue for a trim.

"You're not fine." Ginger grabbed me by my elbows and propelled me toward the full-length mirror hanging from my closet door. "You've got no oomph, no pizzazz."

"I'm not a pizzazz type of person."

"Anybody can have pizzazz. You think those girls on the cover of *Glamour* magazine look good in the morning? It's all sleight of hand. Makeup magic."

Ginger's mama, Ceci, sold Avon in her spare time when she wasn't redecorating their house. She let Ginger have all the free samples she wanted.

"Buddy, do you or do you not want to fit in at high school? You're not in grammar school anymore. You need to stand out from the crowd."

"I guess I do, but that doesn't mean I'm going to go to school with a bowl of fruit on my head."

Ginger narrowed her eyes, which she'd outlined with a purple liner snatched from her mama's Avon sample kit.

"You always exaggerate. All I am suggesting is making a few minor changes to your look."

I hadn't realized I *had* a look. Ginger stood behind me, yanked on my long brown hair, and piled it on top of my head.

"I look stupid."

She let my hair fall back in place. "Listen, I have a great idea." She opened the phone book on my desk, scribbled a number on a notepad and dialed my pink Princess phone using the eraser end of a pencil to protect her nails.

"What are you doing?" She could be so bossy. Like the time she took over my twelfth birthday party, organized a spin-the-bottle game in the mudroom, and charged admission.

Ginger cleared her throat and sucked in her cheeks. "Hello, Hair Palace, I would like to make an appointment for a beauty consultation." She used her Park Avenue accent, the one she faked when she made calls for her mama to tell her customers their Avon orders were ready for pickup. "Yes, Saturday at ten will be fine. My name? Oh, it's Buddy Mullens."

She hung up the phone before I could tell the person at the other end it had all been a mistake, my hair suited me fine, and I didn't need to consult anybody. "I hate it when you do this. Did you ever think maybe I like the way I look?"

Not true. I didn't mind my hair, but I hadn't felt comfortable with my body since sixth grade when it was okay to look like a little girl. Mama told me I was a late bloomer. Most days I didn't mind the way I looked. My outside matched my inside, which was quiet. I could hide in a crowd.

Ginger stood with her hands on her hips. "No, it never occurred to me, Buddy, because you once told me you'll never get a boy to notice you."

"That's okay with me. I'll have enough to worry about in high school without trying to figure out what to do with a boy."

"What about that new boy, Jack? The one you drew a heart next to in your yearbook."

I noticed him right away because he—well, because he was very cute, but mostly because he didn't show off like the other boys. The girls in Teresa Potter's clique, including Teresa, knocked each other out of the way to walk close to him in the hall. I didn't stand a chance.

"He seems nice, but I don't want you to start scheming. What if I tried to help every time you whined about something? I don't need a fairy god-mother."

"I'm your best friend, Buddy. I want you to get invited to the parties. And if Jack Fletcher likes you, you'll have it made."

"Well, I'm not going to follow him around the way you do when you have a crush on someone, like the time you spent an entire Saturday following Brad Vickers."

"I do not follow boys, I do research. Which is what you should be doing with Jack. How will you know what he likes?"

"I know what he likes. Her name is Teresa Potter. He practically drooled when she came into French class."

"What does Teresa Potter have that you haven't got?"

"Long blond hair and breasts."

"Nothing you can't buy for a price."

I stared at my chest in the mirror. There was not much to see. "Mama says hers grew after she graduated from high school."

Ginger smiled as if I had said the funniest thing in the world. "We can't wait that long, Buddy. I'll meet you at the Hair Palace at ten on Saturday."

CHAPTER FIFTEEN

GINGER WAITED on the bench outside the Hair Palace. She jumped up and held out her slender wrist so I could read her watch.

"You're late. It's ten-fifteen. Ruby is waiting on you."

I hoped my appointment had been given away. Didn't I already have enough change in my life without changing the way I looked? Even if Ruby could turn me into a new woman, it would be false advertising. My outside might shout, "I am cool, I am fun," when the truth was closer to, "I am a loser, stay away, contents will explode."

Ginger was in full makeup, her hair sprayed into crisp waves that hung to her shoulders. She wore a starched white middy-blouse over navy-blue pants with big white buttons up the side. "Remember, you don't have to make a decision today. Consider this research."

Ruby Dyer, the lady who gave Mama a frizzy perm every six months, waved to me from the shampoo sink. "Be right with you, Buddy."

Ruby was chubby, but in a healthy-looking way, her skin peaches-and-cream lovely. One year she was my Brownie leader, and she always encouraged me to sing at the top of my lungs even though I sang off-key.

"So what are we doing for you today?" Ruby settled me in the chair at her station and unwound my braids, running her fingers through the tangled hair.

Except for a woman sitting under the dryer, we had the place to ourselves. "This was Ginger's idea. She thinks I need a new look."

Ginger smiled from across the room where she sat flipping through old issues of *Seventeen* magazine. "She needs some oomph, Ruby. How about this?" She walked over and showed us a photo of a girl wearing a sleek, shoulder-length pageboy.

"What do you think, Buddy?" Ruby asked as she brushed out my hair.

"I think that hairdo would take a lot of work and be too short to get into braids."

Ginger bounced off to the card table near the back of the shop, where Ruby had set out coffee and pastries. She helped herself to a cup of black coffee. I think it made her feel sophisticated.

Ruby leaned down until her face was close to mine, her mouth a breath from my ear. "How's your mama, sweet girl? Doing all right?"

Our eyes met in the mirror and I sensed she knew the truth about Mama. "She's doing fine, Ruby, she's A-OK."

"That's good. That's real good to hear. You say hey for me when you see her and tell her Ruby makes house calls. Anything she needs—wash, set, cut. I'll be happy to fix her up."

Ruby suggested maybe what I needed was a wash and conditioning treatment to get the town pool's chlorine out of my hair. She cut an inch of dead ends from the bottom and sat me under the dryer long enough for me to read a *Saturday Evening Post* cover to cover.

When it was dry, Ruby brushed out my hair until it gleamed like polished chestnuts, swept up the sides, and anchored them with sparkly green butterfly barrettes she kept in a glass display case at the front of the shop.

"These are a little gift from me to you," she said as she snapped them in place. "You're a good girl, Buddy. Don't you be forgetting that."

Ruby wouldn't let me pay for anything, saying Mama had helped her out more times then she could count.

It was almost lunchtime, so we headed over to Walton's Soda Shop, to get grilled cheese sandwiches and chocolate shakes. We could have eaten for free at my daddy's place, but Ginger liked Walton's, because that's where the high-school kids hung out. She especially liked to steal quick glances at the athletes who stretched out their overgrown bodies in the red-vinyl booths as they consumed huge platters of juicy cheeseburgers and homemade french fries slathered in ketchup.

We took the last booth, the one next to the jukebox, with Ginger facing the door. I was content to be hidden away, unseen. I didn't need anyone gawking at me and asking what did I do to my hair. Not that Ruby did anything drastic, but I wasn't used to looking so slick on a Saturday.

We were halfway through our chocolate shakes when Ginger let out a gasp. "I just had the best idea. We'll get you a wig. It will be so cool. That way you can keep your stupid braids."

"Forget it." I reached up and played with the butterfly barrettes. "This is as fancy as I get."

She shook her head in disgust. "Hear me out. Just imagine you show up on the first day of school as a blonde. Buddy, you need something to make you stand out if you want to get invited to the parties. The important ones they have after the football games."

"Why? Give me one good reason." Wasn't Mama being in the loony bin enough of a burden to carry? Did I need fake hair to set myself apart from the normal kids who had a mama at home to pack their lunches and send them off to school with warnings to be good and study hard?

Ginger flipped her hair behind her shoulders. "Will you listen to me for once? High school is going to be the best time of our life, and I plan to be at those parties, every one of them. So if you're my friend, you'll try harder."

I dropped the spoon I was using to ladle out the shake; it clanged against my dish. "Okay, I'll try to fit in, but no wig. I wore one last Halloween and it felt like I had a small animal on my head."

Ginger laughed, and I noticed she had a piece of cheese caught in her teeth. For an instant, I felt mean enough to let her smile her way out of Walton's looking like she had a gold tooth, but Ginger was my friend and I needed to keep her.

"You have cheese between your teeth," I told her, and she immediately panicked and ran for the bathroom.

I was working on my fries when I heard the bell of the front door jangle, followed by the sound of catcalls and people laughing. I peeked around the side of the booth. Verna paused near the door with her baby sister, Jane, perched on her hip, Russell at her side, and Tammy bringing up the rear. Russell waved at the kids sitting at the counter, as if they were his friends and glad to see him. Verna noticed me and pushed Russell toward the back of the store.

"I've been looking all over for you. Where you been?" Verna wore a purple circle skirt with a green blouse and green kneesocks. She resembled a giant eggplant. A skinny one. Jane laughed at Russell as he made spit balls from paper napkins and blew them against the wall.

"Stop that, Russell, and sit down." Verna wedged him between the two of us and balanced Jane on her lap. Tammy played with the buttons on the jukebox.

"Can I have your french fries, Buddy?" Russell stuffed a few in his mouth without waiting for my permission.

"What's the emergency?" I was hoping Verna would be gone before Ginger came back. I didn't mind sitting in Walton's with the Sanford tribe, but it might cause Ginger to have a conniption.

"Our daddy's missing. Been gone two days, and that's not like him."

"Did he go to the cockfights in Kerryville?"

"That was day before yesterday. He usually has too much to drink and has to stay over, but he's always back by lunch the next day. He says we don't have the brains to run the dump. He thinks people will rob us blind if he's not around."

"Maybe you should call the police."

Verna let Jane suck on a fry soaked with ketchup. "I did. That's where I've come from, the police station."

"Did you fill out a missing-person's report?"

"Sergeant Peters, you know, the one who came to visit us in third grade? He was at the front desk, and he said he can't do anything for forty-eight hours. Come back tomorrow, he told me."

"But, it's been that long already."

"He said forty-eight hours from the time he was expected back. What should I do, Buddy?"

"I guess you'll have to wait."

"No, I mean if he never comes home. What will I do?" She looked over at Russell, who had lost interest in the food and was back to shooting spit-balls.

I offered her a drink of my shake. "Don't worry, he'll show up. He always does." If he were my daddy, I'd be praying he had fallen off the face of the earth, but maybe I'd be singing a different tune if I were left in charge of those kids.

"This time feels different, Buddy." Her eyes filled with tears. I'd never seen Verna cry, not even when Jimmy Miller knocked her off the swing on the playground and she opened up her knee so bad she needed stitches.

I fed Jane another fry and squeezed Verna's hand. "I'll ask my daddy to help. He'll know what to do."

Russell put two straws up his nose. "Look, Verna, I'm a walrus."

Verna removed the straws. "Come over later if you can, Buddy. Before it gets dark." She smoothed her skirt and readjusted Jane on her other hip. "We can play Scrabble."

"I'll try. But I can't promise, so don't be waiting for me." If Verna's daddy went off on a toot, he'd be meaner than a snake when he got home.

"Try hard, Buddy." Verna held tight to Russell's hand as she led him through Walton's and out to the sidewalk. She yelled to Tammy to get a move on.

"Are they gone?" Ginger hissed at me from the doorway to the ladies' room.

"Have you been standing there all this time? I thought you were redoing your makeup."

Ginger slid into the booth opposite me. "I don't want to sound mean or anything, but hanging out with Verna is not going to get you invited parties. Did you see the way those boys acted when they saw her?"

"That's because of Russell. They torture him at school. He can't help the way he is."

"You're wrong, Buddy, it's not just because of Russell. Did you see what she was wearing? And those awful shoes. She holds them together with rubber bands. If I had to dress like that, I'd hide in my house."

I thought of Verna and her eggplant outfit, her long, skinny legs holding her up like the stakes of pole beans, the soles of her loafers flapping as she walked tall, balancing a baby on her hip and hanging on to her demented brother for dear life. Verna Kaye Sanford was the bravest person I knew.

CHAPTER SIXTEEN

 NEEDED TO talk to Daddy about Verna in private, so I told Ginger I had to help close up the drugstore. Ginger promised to call me after dinner.

Darlene looked busy making ice-cream sundaes for two ladies who wore fancy hats with veils. She waved to me as I moved toward the back of the store. Daddy stood behind the pharmacy counter entering figures in a ledger. "Why, Buddy, what brings you to town?"

"Ginger and I went to Walton's." He didn't seem to notice my new hairdo, so I didn't mention she also dragged me to the Hair Palace against my will.

175

"Glad to see you getting out with your friends. No sense you moping around the house." He hung up his white jacket on a brass hook. "I think I'll leave early today. Darlene can lock up."

"Hey, Daddy, didn't you tell me I should always come to you if I have a problem?"

He paused at the back door, his hand on the knob. "Something wrong, Buddy? Didn't it go well today with your mama? You know I warned you. . . ."

"No Daddy, it's not Mama, it's Verna. Her daddy's missing."

He sighed and motioned me through the door, closing it behind us. "Parker Sanford is not the world's most reliable man. He's been known to drink a little and disappear for a day or two. I know Verna is your friend, but it's really none of our business."

"Verna's all alone, Daddy. With those kids and her mama laid up in bed. Can't we do something?"

We stopped next to the Buick. "Hop in, Buddy." He took off before I could protest and we were almost home when he made a U-turn and backtracked to River Road.

"Thanks, Daddy." We listened to the ball game on the radio as we drove to Verna's.

"I haven't done anything yet. Rina Sanford is a private woman. She won't take kindly to my sticking my nose where it doesn't belong."

Daddy got that right. Two minutes after we parked in front of their house, Rina found the strength to pull herself from bed and roll her wobbly wheelchair to the front porch. Her bushy red hair looked sharp as steel wool. She wore a long cotton dress, limp against her legs withered from the polio.

Rina cleared her throat. "Unless you've got business at the dump, I'll thank you to get off my property."

The two of us stood at the bottom of the steps, me behind Daddy, using him for a shield. He removed a white handkerchief from his back pocket and wiped his brow.

"Mrs. Sanford, I came to offer my help until your husband returns. Buddy told me your girl Verna seemed concerned about his whereabouts."

Rina reached down to pick up one of the kids'

shoes and threw it at a squirrel stealing nuts from the ground. "Don't need no help." She said this loud enough for Verna to hear from where she stood just inside the screened door. "Verna's brought you out here on a fool's errand."

Daddy tried to tell her he'd check back with the police, but she turned her chair around, wheeled herself inside the house and slammed the door shut.

Verna peered through the screen, her face bare of expression. Daddy signaled me to get into the car. I walked down the slope to the road, but not before giving a little wave to Verna.

In spite of Rina's warning to stay out of their affairs, Daddy and I went back to town to police headquarters. Sergeant Peters made a few sympathetic sounds from a mouth filled with coffee and doughnuts.

"Hold on a minute," Sergeant Peters called to us as we retraced our steps across the lobby, Daddy holding tight to my hand. "Doesn't Parker Sanford run those cockfights in Kerryville?"

Daddy started to say we knew nothing about

any cockfights, but I put my hand on his arm to silence him and turned to face Sergeant Peters.

"Yes, sir, I believe you're right. Verna, she's his daughter, said he went there day before yesterday. He took off with his truck loaded up with those poor animals he keeps behind the dump. I saw them one day. He puts sharp spurs around their little ankles so they can claw each other." I demonstrated this by pretending to jab at his arm with my fingernails. "Verna says sometimes they fight to the death."

Daddy shook his head in disgust. "Well, it's not legal in these parts."

"I know that, but Verna says people bet lots of money and her daddy gets to keep some of it."

Sergeant Peters held up a finger. "I've got an idea." He picked up the phone on the counter and dialed. "This is Sergeant Peters of the Moodus police. We've got a missing person name of Sanford, Parker Sanford. Yes, I'll wait," he said to the person on the other end of the line.

Daddy gave my hand a reassuring squeeze. All I could manage was a nervous smile.

Sergeant Peters nodded his head. "Yes, I'm

179

here," he said into the phone. "That doesn't surprise me. Thanks for your help. I'll let his family know."

He hung up the phone. "I've found Parker Sanford."

"Where is he?" I moved closer to the sergeant's desk. "Is he all right?"

Sergeant Peters laughed. "He's doing fine. Got himself a suite at the Kerryville Police Station. Seems he was arrested for gambling and animal cruelty and couldn't come up with the bail money."

"How long does he have to stay in jail?" I thought of Verna waiting for word of her daddy at home, trying to hold everything together.

"He can get out as soon as he pays the fifty-dollar fine. Otherwise he gets himself a one week vacation in the Kerryville jail."

"What happened to the birds?" I hated to think of them running wild, left to starve to death.

"A bunch of ladies from the ASPCA showed up and rescued them. That must have been a sight, them gals carting off a heap of bloody birds in their station wagons."

"Thanks for the help." Daddy gave Sergeant

Peters a quick salute and told me to come on, our business was done.

I had to run to catch up with him. "We can't leave Mr. Sanford in jail."

"It's not our concern, Buddy. We'll stop by and tell Mrs. Sanford her husband's all right and set her mind to rest."

"But he's stuck there. Parker Sanford is stuck in jail unless someone bails him out."

"He'll be out in a week. That's what the sergeant said. Maybe it'll do him good to suffer the consequences of what he's done."

"But, Daddy, it's Verna who's going to suffer the most." I hated to think what the kids in town would say to her and Russell when they got wind of their daddy being arrested. "There must be something we can do."

"They're private people, Buddy. We'll do more harm if we interfere."

He started up the car and we rode in silence, my mind spinning faster than a windmill in a hurricane. I had never known anyone who went to jail. Not that Mr. Sanford and I were on friendly terms; he mostly kept to himself, sifting through the piles of garbage hoping to find treasure, burning what was useless in great sooty fires. I pictured him in a tiny cell, cursing a blue streak about losing his birds.

Did he even think about his family waiting on him at home? Or did he lie there on a narrow cot with threadbare sheets feeling sorry for himself?

My thoughts turned to Mama, closed off from her own family at Moodus Meadows, and of Verna's mama, Rina, who shut herself off from the world. Why did they give up on themselves? When did they forsake all hope of mattering?

"Drop me off, Daddy. I'd rather break the news to Verna by myself. She might be embarrassed in front of you."

He slowed the car and came to a stop in the clearing in front of the Sanfords' house. "You sure about this, Buddy? I can wait out here."

"No, you go on. I'll stay awhile with Verna. Maybe play a game of Scrabble with her to take her mind off her troubles."

"Be home before dark." He drove off slow enough for me to catch him if I changed my mind.

Verna came outside as soon as Daddy's Buick moved out of sight. "You staying over? Where's your stuff?"

"I can't sleep over. Let's go in the tent. I need to tell you something." Russell, Tammy, and Jane watched us from the windows, opaque with finger smears.

"Russell, don't let Jane get into trouble," Verna shouted. "Tammy, you keep an eye on Russell."

I opened the flap to the tent and ushered her inside. "Take a seat," I requested, as if it were my tent and I was the hostess.

"What's the big deal?" Verna sat on the sleeping bag, her knees pulled up to her chest. "Do you have some news about my daddy?"

There was no way to sugarcoat the fact her daddy was in jail. "We found him. He's okay."

In spite of my reassurance that her daddy had not died in a fiery car wreck, Verna's face blanched to a shade of rice paper. "Where is he, Buddy?"

"He's in the Kerryville jail. He got himself arrested for holding cockfights and gambling. Some ladies from the ASPCA took away his birds and he can't get out for a week unless he pays the fine."

"How much is it?" Verna stood and paced around the small tent, ducking her head each time she approached a corner.

"Fifty dollars." I tried to remember how much babysitting money I had stashed in my sock drawer. "I can give you twelve."

"Thanks, Buddy. That leaves thirty-eight. We've got twenty in a tin in the kitchen, but that's for groceries. I have a little something put away for a rainy day." She pulled back the sleeping bag and revealed a hole, covered by loose dirt, a cigar box wedged just below the surface. I watched her count out nine one-dollar bills. "Okay, now we need twenty-nine dollars."

"Even if you can't come up with the money, Sergeant Peters said they'd let your daddy go free in five more days. But he'll still have to pay the fine when he has his day in court."

"I want him home today, Buddy. Mama needs him. She gets so lonely with just me and the kids. He reads to her every night and makes her feel safe."

It never occurred to me that anyone would pine for Parker Sanford. Maybe I had misjudged the man. Could it be I was losing my powers of observation? Hadn't I missed the signs in Mama?

If I was to help her, I needed time to think, to be alone. She believed it was her fault Booth had died. Anyone could have told her that was a load of poppycock, but she wouldn't listen, couldn't be swayed from the thought that she had caused his death. Those doctors and nurses at Moodus Meadows could give her all the pills and therapy they wanted; I knew she'd never get better until I could prove to her that she was wrong. What could I say, what were the perfect words that would release her from her guilt? There had to be an answer.

I helped Verna rebury the cigar box. "I have to get home," I said, and stood to go.

She remained kneeling on the sleeping bag, but held on to my wrist. "Will you come back?"

"Of course, I'm going to get that babysitting money for you."

She shook her head and sighed. "No you ain't, Buddy. You're never coming back and I can't blame you. Your parents won't let you be friends with me anymore because my daddy's a jailbird." Her eyes filled with tears and she turned away, her hand still holding on to me for dear life.

"That's the stupidest thing I've ever heard you say. What kind of friend do you think I am? One of those fair-weather kind?"

"But your mama and daddy won't want you hanging around a criminal's daughter." She bit her lip and released her grip on me.

"Sit down, Verna. I've got something to tell you."

She lowered herself to the ground, the whole time keeping me in her sights as if this was a trick and I'd disappear the minute she turned away. The way we sometimes did to Russell when he was being a pest.

"Verna, your daddy's not the only one who's locked away. My mama's real sad, and she's living in Moodus Meadows for a while."

Verna's mouth with its upturned corners remained still; her eyes grew tender with sympathy. She moved close to me and held my hand, not tight as if she feared I might run away, but softly, a gesture of friendship, of acceptance.

"Tell me, Buddy, tell me everything," she said, and I knew in a moment of crystal clarity that I could tell Verna anything, anything at all. Maybe that was what drew me to this sad-looking girl, a comfort even I didn't recognize until then. With Verna, I didn't have to pretend, I could be exactly who I was, Buddy Mullens.

Leaning against a pile of pillows in the musty old tent, I unburdened my heart to Verna Kaye Sanford. All the words I'd kept inside me, all the worries, all the regrets, I let tumble from my lips. The truths about Mama and my family filled the tent, but somehow the air felt lighter, and I could breathe easy.

After I'd said my piece, Verna hugged me and whispered, "Best friends forever."

"Best friends forever," I whispered back to her.

CHAPTER SEVENTEEN

"I'VE GOT A plan to get your daddy home," I told Verna after we finished off half a bag of marshmallows and some chocolate milk.

She pressed the money from the cigar box into my hand and lent me her bike. I tore along River Road, the tall pines a blur. *Please let Sherry be home,* I prayed. Maybe I couldn't get Mama out of Moodus Meadows just yet, but I wasn't about to let the small obstacle of twenty-nine dollars keep Parker Sanford from his family.

Daddy sat on the porch glider reading the paper. "You didn't stay very long. How did they take the news?"

"Good, real good." I had no time to explain what really happened. "Is Sherry home?"

Daddy's newspaper rattled as he folded it back to the sports page. "I think she's getting ready to go out. She said something about seeing a movie. Where'd you get that bike?"

"It's Verna's." I ran inside and found Sherry in my room putting the finishing touches to her makeup. She'd fixed her hair bouffant style, copied from a magazine photo of Jacqueline Kennedy, the wife of the senator running for president.

"Hey, Buddy. There's some tuna salad and a lemon-and-carrot Jell-O mold in the refrigerator for your dinner." She gave me a big smile. "I'm going to the movies with Darren and afterward we're going back to his place. For dessert."

"Oh, that's nice." I flopped on my bed, nonchalant, as if I didn't have a care in the world.

"What's got you all sweated up?" She pointed at me with her mascara wand.

"I rode all the way home from Verna's in record time. Didn't stop once."

"What do you think about Darren inviting me to his place? Think he's getting serious?"

"Maybe."

"You don't look real happy for me." Sherry nudged me with her bare foot. "What's the matter? Thinking about your mama?"

"Not exactly. It's Verna. Her daddy's in jail and she needs fifty dollars to get him out, actually twenty-nine because I have twelve dollars baby-sitting money she can have. . . ."

"Whoa. You're about to bust a gut. Slow down and tell me one more time what you need all this money for."

We sat on the bed, and Sherry listened while I filled her in about the cockfights and the gambling and how Rina Sanford needed Parker home to take care of her.

"Maybe he's not as scary as I thought. It sounds like he's real kind to his wife. Could you lend me the rest of the money? I'll pay you back."

Sherry slipped on her shoes and pulled me to my feet. "Buddy, the man looks mean as a junkyard dog, not anyone I'd care to meet in a dark alley, but he is Verna's daddy, so who am I to judge? I think we've got enough time if we hurry. I'll call Darren and tell him to meet me at the theater so we don't miss the start of the show."

"You stay here." Sherry pointed to where I sat in the front seat of her Impala. I watched her sashay up the brick steps of the Kerryville police headquarters, swinging her white leather purse on its gold chain, her hips shifting east and west.

Ten minutes later she returned, climbed in the car, and drove off before I could say boo.

"Where's Verna's daddy? Wouldn't they let him out?"

"It's all taken care of, sweetie. I paid the fine. The man at the front desk said he'd do the paperwork and have Parker Sanford on his way home within the hour. I told the officer to keep it a secret where the money came from."

Sherry didn't want to keep Darren waiting, saying there were dozens of women who would scoop him up faster than hawks on a field mouse. There was no time to take me home, but Darren didn't seem to mind me tagging along.

191

Before the lights went down, I scanned the theater. I was sort of hoping to see Jack Fletcher, but I didn't want him to be with a girl. That would have about broken my heart. Not that I had a chance with such a fine boy, but as long as he didn't have a girl, I could dream.

"Who are you looking for, Buddy?" Sherry leaned close, her lipstick glistening.

"Nobody." The less said the better.

"It wouldn't be Jack Fletcher you're craning your neck to see?"

"Who told you?"

"Ginger. She let it slip when I came to his photo in the yearbook and said he was cute. 'That's what Buddy thinks, too,' Ginger said."

I slumped in my seat, and the lights dimmed before she could see me blush.

During the movie, I stared straight ahead so I wouldn't have to watch Sherry and Darren smooching. It didn't help. Wherever I looked, couples in love sat scrunched together attached at the lips.

I tried to concentrate on the movie, *A Summer*

Place. Troy Donahue, a handsome blond movie star, kissed Sandra Dee, a beautiful blonde with eyes as warm as brown velvet. During the closeup, their lips filled the screen.

In the story, Sandra and Troy fell in love in spite of Troy's daddy being an alcoholic, Sandra's mama ranting and raving like a wild woman when she thought her baby girl did the dirty deed with Troy, and Sandra's daddy declaring his love for Troy's mama in the boathouse where they went to be alone. They almost made my family seem normal.

I tried to imagine Jack kissing me the way Troy kissed Sandra; the thought made me feel as if my veins were filled with fizzy water. Could I ever be like Sherry or Ginger, fretting over my hair and makeup, penciling *Date with Jack* on my calendar? The way my life was going, how could I ever believe in happy endings?

CHAPTER EIGHTEEN

*I*T SEEMED ONLY right to give the Sanfords some privacy after their daddy's return, but I was pressed for time.

The day after Sherry and I bailed Verna's daddy out of jail, I sat on the front porch, my dog Pepper at my side, my mind in a pickle. I'd promised Mama to handle the costumes for her play, but I couldn't do it alone. I needed Verna's help. A little past noon, it dawned on me Verna might mistake my respect for her family's privacy as rejection.

"She'll be happy to see me," I said to Pepper, who ignored me, and snapped at a flea hopping on his back.

★ ★ ★

For once Verna didn't have a kid hanging off her
elbow. She sat alone on the porch steps shucking
corn.

"Where is everybody?"

"Daddy took Mama and the kids to the market.
Somebody bailed Daddy out of jail last night. I
think I know who."

"I had help. Sherry came up with the rest of the
money, but she said it's best not to tell your daddy.
Let him think his luck is changing."

Verna handed me an ear of corn. I ripped
away the husk and dumped it into a brown-paper
bag. "Tell Sherry I promise I'll pay her back one
day."

"Okay, I'll tell her. But she won't hold you to it.
Hey, Verna, want to help with a play?" There, I had
said it, that wasn't so hard.

She stopped what she was doing. "What kind of
play?"

"A musical. *Oklahoma!* You can be the costume
designer."

"What's the catch?" She rubbed her fingers

together turning the silky corn floss into thread.

"We have to use your sewing machine."

"Who's going to be in the play?"

"Mama and her friends." I said this nonchalantly, as if putting on a play with people in Moodus Meadows was an everyday occurrence.

If I'd asked Ginger, she would have made up a flimsy excuse, pretended she was going to be busy polishing the family silver for the rest of the year. But Verna was not Ginger. She nodded her head, yes. "Sounds like fun. I've always wanted a chance to design something fancy. When do we start?"

I jumped to my feet. "Right now, this very minute. They already made posters saying the show is Saturday after next." I figured the sooner we put on the show, the quicker Mama'd think her work was done and get herself home where she belonged.

"Holy mackerel. That gives us ten days."

"You can do it, Verna. I know you can. We'll do the sewing here and I'll keep an eye on the kids for you."

Verna got the biggest smile on her face. "You sure you know what you're letting yourself in for, Buddy? Russell alone is a handful."

"Piece of cake," I said.

For the next ten days, we worked nonstop. Gram donated fabric from her stash, mostly calicos and gingham. Daddy gave Verna and me five dollars to spend on fringe, ribbon, and other doodads.

Verna sewed at the kitchen table, fabric flying over the machine's feed dogs faster than a sled over packed snow. I cooked, cleaned, and looked after her brother and sisters, losing Tammy once for an hour, but locating her asleep in Verna's tent, her face smeared with chocolate.

Rina seemed to get used to having me around. She stayed out of bed a little more each day, sitting in a rocker by the window, her head bent low, doing the hand stitching on the dresses and bonnets. Verna's daddy came in each day at noon to check on the lot of us and to fix us peanut-butter-and-jelly sandwiches, and ketchup sandwiches when those ran out. Up close, he looked kinder, and he didn't smell bad, considering he spent most of his day knee-deep in rubbish.

Two days before the play, we went to Moodus Meadows to do the final fittings. We found everyone assembled in the auditorium. I was forced to shout to be heard above the sounds of hammers banging and backdrops being scraped across the stage.

"Where's my mama?" I asked.

"Over here, Buddy." Mama knelt on a drop cloth, painting wooden trees. She put down her paintbrush and waved to us.

"Are those the costumes?" She pointed to the shopping bags we carried.

Verna passed one of the bags to her. Mama wiped her hands on her overalls, reached inside, and pulled out a dress. She held it up, turning it this way and that, inspecting the stitches, fingering the trim.

"These are gorgeous. Verna, you could be a Hollywood designer like the ones who make gowns for Audrey Hepburn."

"Thanks, Mrs. Mullens. Buddy and my mama

helped." The cast stopped rehearsing and tried on their outfits for the show. Using a needle and thread from her sewing kit, Verna nipped and tucked every seam and gusset until everyone looked band-box perfect.

Mama perched on the edge of the stage, nodding her approval. She rose to her feet, dashed across the glossy floor and hugged us to her. "You girls are the best. How can I ever thank you?"

I ached to tell her, *Come home right now, this very minute,* but I kept quiet and hugged her back.

CHAPTER NINETEEN

*T*HE DAY OF the show arrived, and somehow we managed to get everything ready. Well, almost everything. There were a few loose ends, but everyone at Moodus Meadows pitched in to help.

I found Mama backstage, along with Sherry. They were struggling with a giant fake cactus plant. Mama looked up from her chore. "Where's your daddy?"

"He's in the audience."

"Already?" Mama looked at her watch. "We don't start for an hour."

"Tess wanted to get a good seat." Sherry rolled

her eyes and glued a false mustache on one of the cowboys.

Mama peeked between the curtains. "Gram's knees will stiffen up if she sits that long. Buddy, go get her and bring her back here where she can put up her feet."

"Oh, no, not me. Tess will have a hissy fit if she loses those front-row seats."

Mama pushed me through the opening in the curtain. "Tess can save those seats if she wants them so badly. Now, you go get Gram and tell her I have a chaise back here for her to rest on. It's an old one from the swimming pool, but it's good enough."

I took a short flight of stairs off the side of the stage, and took a seat between Gram and Tess. Daddy occupied himself with an old copy of *Reader's Digest*.

"Mama wants Gram to come backstage and put her feet up. She says her knees will stiffen if she sits here too long."

Tess leaned toward Gram. "She's fine right where she is, aren't you, Mama?" Tess unwrapped a Tootsie Roll and offered me a section.

"The play doesn't begin for an hour. Mama's afraid Gram's knees will seize up. You know, because of her arthritis."

"I heard you the first time, Buddy. I don't need you reminding me about her knees." Tess set her mouth in a tight line.

"Sorry, but Mama's worried about Gram sitting in this old folding chair."

Tess crossed her legs, swinging the top one faster and faster until it seemed her foot might fly off. "This place isn't doing Ellen any good if she's still trying to be the boss and control everyone else's life. Maybe she should worry about herself for a change."

"Hush up, Tess." Gram leaned on Daddy's shoulder and pushed herself off her chair. "I don't want to sit here and I don't want to sit backstage. I think I'll walk around a bit, get myself some fresh air. You people act as if I don't have the brains God gave a chicken."

"But, Mama," Tess protested. "Someone will want your seat."

"If you want to save it, fine. Otherwise I'll find myself someplace else to sit. I don't think this will be a standing-room-only production."

"Hey, Buddy, you're needed backstage. We have a slight problem with one of the costumes." Sherry held a corsage of makeup brushes in her hand.

I followed her to Yvonne, who'd split a seam on her dress.

I examined the frayed edges of the gingham. "Where's Verna? She can mend it for her."

Sherry waved the makeup brushes around as if she were painting a scene for me. "Verna's got her hands full." She handed a needle and thread to me.

"What if my stitches fall out when Yvonne's dancing?"

"Here, give that dress to me." Gram stood in the wings of the stage. She removed her hat, gloves and purse and set them on a trunk. "I could repair that dress with my eyes closed."

"So close your eyes and get sewing, Hazel." Sherry tossed her the torn dress. I passed over the needle and thread with relief. Gram fixed the dress in no time with small, even stitches. She bit off the thread and tied a knot.

"Good as new," declared Yvonne. "Thanks so much."

Rustling sounds filtered through the stage curtains as people began to fill the auditorium.

If someone had predicted this was how I was going to spend my summer vacation, I would have told them they were crazy, but there I stood, amazed at what we'd accomplished in a short space of time.

Mama seemed happier than I'd seen her in months. An image of a smiling Mama sitting at her place at our kitchen table played on my mind.

After the last family meeting, I'd overheard Dr. Bueller tell Daddy that she could leave Moodus Meadows as soon as the next week.

"Pinch me, Verna."

Verna narrowed her eyes at me. "What are you talking about, Buddy?"

"I'm so happy. Mama's doing well and you know what that means."

"She gets out of here?" Verna whispered this as if saying it out loud might spoil things.

"Yes. I'll bet she'll be home by next week, maybe sooner." It might have been the day before Christmas, my heart swelled so with anticipation.

CHAPTER TWENTY

*E*VERYONE AGREED Maple Cottage's revival of *Oklahoma!* was a success. Verna and I basked in the glow of fame for most of Saturday. We treated ourselves to the movies on Saturday night with Russell, Tammy, and Jane in tow. Finding seats together in the balcony, Verna made Russell promise not to throw popcorn on the people below us.

Daddy gave us enough time after the movie to go to Walton's for Cokes and fries. He picked us up at ten. Sherry stayed out late with Darren, so I had my room to myself.

It took forever to fall asleep that night. Each time I started to doze off I thought of Mama's homecoming. Maybe we could swim at the pool or picnic by the lake before she had to get ready to return to her job as a guidance counselor at Moodus High School. It was hard to believe I'd be there too.

Dr. Bueller called on Monday morning and talked to Daddy. I loitered near the phone, but Daddy did little more than nod his head and say, "Is that so," every now and then.

He replaced the receiver in the phone cradle, gently, as if it were made of spun glass. "Now, Buddy," he said, and I knew before he uttered another word that Mama had taken a turn for the worse.

"But she seemed so happy, like her old self, you said so, Daddy." What could have happened in two days?

"Don't go getting in a tizzy. It's not as bad as before, just a small setback. Dr. Bueller's got it under control."

Sherry walked up behind me and squeezed my shoulder. "What's his plan?" she asked.

Daddy poured himself another cup of coffee and carried it to the kitchen table, where he sat and stirred in spoon after spoon of sugar until I covered the cup with my hand. I'd spent so much time focusing on Mama, I failed to see how tired he looked, bags under his eyes, his normally pink-skinned face sallow, the life gone out of him.

I squeezed next to him on the edge of his chair. "What should we do?"

He leaned over and kissed the top of my head. "I don't know anymore. Dr. Bueller said a lot of the patients have a setback right before they leave. They get used to the safe environment of Moodus Meadows."

"It's their own world," said Sherry. She joined us at the table, cutting me a thick slab of crumb cake and one for herself. "But somebody has to push them out of their nest or they'll never leave."

Daddy drained his coffee cup and placed it on its saucer; his shaking hand caused it to rattle. "Dr. Bueller thinks a one-day pass might be just what your mama needs. A jump start so to speak."

"You mean have her come home for a day?" I'd take anything I could get.

"Coming home might be more than she's ready to attempt. Dr. Bueller said think of it as a long outing to get Mama used to being away from Moodus Meadows, but with the security of knowing she'll be returning there."

Sherry nodded in approval. "That makes sense. Sort of ease Ellen back into the real world. So when do we pick her up?"

"Wednesday. That will give her time to get used to the idea. We're not supposed to see her until then. And when we do see her, the doctor says we shouldn't talk about her coming home. She might feel we're pressuring her."

Twenty-eight times. In two days, that's how often I called Mama. Each time I hung up the phone before it could ring. Daddy said Dr. Bueller had made all the arrangements, and we could pick up Mama before lunch and take her out for the afternoon.

On Wednesday, I woke up before the sun and lay in my bed listening to Sherry kicking at the sheets, the cotton fabric snapping with each twist and turn of her long legs. There was no way I could fall back to sleep, so I slipped from my bed and tiptoed to the bathroom. I sat on the toilet and daydreamed about getting Mama away from Moodus Meadows, if only for the afternoon. Trying to pass the time, I ran a bath for myself, letting the water run in slowly, its color tinted pink by a handful of Sherry's apple-blossom bath beads.

Soaking in the warm, frothy water, my eyes closed, I willed myself to calm down. *In just a few hours, you'll be with Mama, on the outside, in the real world.*

The sound of Daddy's voice and the muffled reply of Sherry caused me to sit up; the water sloshed over the side of the tub. What were they doing up so early?

I climbed out of the tub and wrapped myself in Mama's terry robe, the one she left hanging on the door. I passed Daddy's room; it stood empty, the bed already made up.

Sherry sat at the kitchen table, sipping from a bottle of Coke. "It's too hot for coffee," she said, and patted the chair next to her.

"What were you and Daddy talking about? Is Mama okay?"

"As far as I know, she's fine and dandy."

"Then why were you two whispering? And where's Daddy?"

Sherry hesitated for a second, but that was long enough to alert me something was wrong. I jumped from my seat, beside myself with confusion.

"Hold on, Buddy, it's not a big deal, just a slight change in plans. We're going to postpone the outing for a couple of days."

"But why?"

"Because your daddy is scared out of his wits that your mama might not be ready."

"Do you believe that?"

Sherry led me to the porch so she could have a cigarette. "You want the truth?"

"That would be nice for a change."

"I think it's your daddy who's not ready to deal with any more upset. You know, in case she has another one of her spells, like she did at the Music Hall. He left for the drugstore before seven. Said he had a lot of paperwork to catch up on."

"But that's not fair. Why should he get to decide?"

"Hey, kiddo, life isn't fair. If it were, I'd be in Hollywood starring in movies with Elvis Presley."

Pepper scratched at the door to be let out. "So now what do we do?"

She stubbed out her cigarette on the porch railing. "I'm supposed to call Moodus Meadows and tell them we'll do this outing on Friday."

"That's two days away. I don't want to wait that long."

"You know, I'd like to help you, but I can't go against your daddy. Besides, there's a big clearance sale at the store and I have to be there by nine to work the counter."

She walked back inside, with me at her heels. She checked the time on the kitchen clock. "It's too early to call, I'll do it when I get to work."

Everyone had some place to go. Even Pepper took off for the neighbor's house to play with their beagle. Alone again, the story of my life. Then it occurred to me being alone might be a blessing in disguise.

"Let me call," I said. "At least I'll be able to talk to Mama."

Sherry stood at the bottom of the stairs, her hand poised on the banister. "You sure?"

"Absolutely, positively."

She smiled at me, relief smoothing her face. "Okay, then. If you get bored, do something fun with Ginger or Verna. I'll leave five dollars on the dresser."

"Thanks, but I won't get bored. There's plenty to do around here."

I wasn't lying about having plenty to keep me busy. If I wanted my plan to work, I needed to get organized. Kidnapping Mama wouldn't be easy, but I was between a rock and a hard place, and the only way out was through the crack in the wall.

CHAPTER TWENTY-ONE

*A*FTER TURNING over couch cushions, going through the pockets of Daddy's trousers, and emptying the sugar bowl on top of the refrigerator, all told I had $17.25. With the five dollars from Sherry, I had enough to treat Mama to a real fine day.

Making myself look sixteen took more effort. An hour in the bathroom with Sherry's makeup bag did the trick. I was especially proud of the way I handled her eyelash-curling contraption, losing only one lash in the process. I placed it in the palm of my hand, made a wish and blew it away. How could

Sherry stand to wear makeup? The mascara weighed down my eyelids and the gooey lipstick caused my lips to slide against each other. I swept back my hair and anchored it in place with a flowered headband.

Clothes were another matter. I pulled one of Sherry's cotton sleeveless shifts over my head. It was way too long, so I hemmed it up with cellophane tape. I added a pair of silver hoop earrings and a long white silk scarf to camouflage my flat chest. I rummaged in Mama's closet and found a pair of beige pumps that I got to fit with a bit of tissue jammed in each toe.

Okay, I told myself, be brave and take a look at yourself. Standing in front of the full-length mirror, I was amazed by the reflection. Not bad, I thought. I put on a pair of Sherry's sunglasses, the white plastic heart-shaped ones, to complete my look.

I left a note on the kitchen table—I'LL BE BACK BY DINNER—in case Daddy came home for lunch. Pepper ignored me when I called him inside, so I let him be and walked quickly to the barn before I lost my nerve.

You can do this, Buddy. Those were Booth's words,

the ones he said to me whenever he let me drive his car and I got scared I'd forgotten everything he taught me.

I slid open the barn door, climbed into the Bel Air and deposited my purse, a straw bag that belonged to Sherry, on the seat. The engine choked a few times before it caught. Easing the car from the barn, I turned my head to see where I was going, one arm draped over the seatback the way Booth showed me. I feared I might crash into something and alert the neighbors who would be sure to call the drugstore and tell on me.

Okay, so far so good. I made it to the corner of our street without any alarms going off, my arms stiff in front of me, my hands at two and ten o'clock on the wheel. Look natural, I whispered under my breath, act as if you do this every day of your life.

There was one traffic light between home and Moodus Meadows and wouldn't you know, it turned red just as I got to the corner. I spotted Darlene on her way to work at the drugstore, waiting to cross the street. *Please don't look this way,* I prayed, but my prayer fell on deaf ears. Just as she got square in front of me, she turned and stared, a puzzled look on her face as if she couldn't quite place where she knew me from. We might have remained there all day, but the light changed and a man in a truck behind me honked his horn, causing Darlene to hightail it to the sidewalk.

Sweat ringed my armpits and I'd chewed off most of my lipstick by the time I got to Moodus Meadows. I left the Bel Air at the edge of the parking lot. If Mama saw Booth's car too soon she might run back inside and lock herself away for good.

I found her in the vegetable garden giving someone advice on the best way to know when the tomatoes were ready to be picked. "Buddy, is that you?" She squinted her eyes and looked me over the way she used to do before I left for Sunday school.

"I decided to dress up."

She smiled at me. "I guess you did. You look like a movie star."

I knew she was just saying that to make me feel good, but it worked. At least she didn't tell me to get myself in the bathroom and scrub my face.

Mama wore her old denim jumper, but she had

on a nice pair of white sandals and her hair looked fashionable, turned under in a pageboy.

"I'll just get my purse," she said. "Where's your daddy?"

"Let me get your purse for you, is it in your room?" I ran ahead of her, ignoring her question.

A minute later, she stood waiting by the door, the strap of her white leather bag clutched in her hand, while I signed her out in a little book left on a table in the lobby. Next to when she'd be back, I wrote NEVER.

"I can't stay out too long," she said. "That's what I told your daddy." She looked around the parking lot. "Where is he?"

"He's in the car." I tried to move her along before she could change her mind.

She spotted the Bel Air and froze in place. "That looks like Booth's car."

"It surely does. Let's take a look at it," I suggested in a soothing voice as if we were at a car dealership and in the market to buy a new vehicle. "It can't hurt."

She spun around, still looking for Daddy; I began

to panic. "Come on, Mama. Let's have a look. I'll bet it's not as well-kept as Booth's."

This peaked her interest. She peered inside the open window. "This is Booth's car, isn't it, Buddy?"

"Now, don't get mad at us, but the Buick's in the shop and the battery in your car went dead. Daddy had no choice. He didn't want to disappoint you and cancel our outing."

"It would have been fine with me. Where is he, anyway?"

"He said he had to talk to someone in the billing office about something, but he told me to get you so we could leave as soon as he finished up."

With great reluctance, Mama got into the car, touching the dashboard with her fingertips. I didn't waste a minute getting myself into the driver's seat.

"What do you think you're doing?"

"I'll just sit here so we can chat while we're waiting for Daddy."

Her eyes darted from side to side; her fingers pumped up and down as if she were playing a piano. I was trying to act casual, gossiping about Sherry and Ginger and anything else that came into my head to calm her down, when I spotted Dr. Bueller walking across the lawn. Each stride of his long legs caused my heart to beat faster. I put my plan into red alert.

I turned the key too hard; it let out a sharp, grinding sound. Slipping the car into gear, I sped out of the parking lot, waving to the doctor so he wouldn't think I had anything to hide. He waved back, doing a double take as he realized it was Buddy Mullens at the wheel.

"Stop the car!" Mama yelled at me, her back pressed tight against the seat, her hand clutching the armrest as if she were on the loop-the-loop ride at the carnival.

"We're going to have an adventure," I yelled over the roar of the engine. I turned the car onto the highway and headed for the shopping center where Sherry worked. I kept my eyes on the road, drove ten miles under the speed limit.

"When did you learn to drive?" Her voice sounded calmer, less like she wanted to jump from the car.

"Booth taught me."

I heard Mama's breath catch in her throat, but she remained quiet, patting my arm gently as I spoke. It was wonderful to have her all to myself, to have her attention.

I told her about Booth giving me secret driving lessons after she and Daddy went to sleep. She smiled when I got to the part about us parking the Bel Air in the back field with the top down, gazing at the night sky, Booth pointing to the Big Dipper.

"You're a good driver, Buddy," was all she said before she closed her eyes and listened to me talk for the rest of the ride.

CHAPTER TWENTY-TWO

CARS COMPETING for spaces clogged the parking lot of the Town and Country shopping center. Red-faced people sat hunched over the steering wheels of their cars circling the lot in ninety-degree heat. Nobody looked happy to be shopping, even though the signs in the windows promised the biggest sales of the year.

"Maybe this isn't a good day to shop." Mama pointed to the exit as if she had had enough and was ready to leave.

"Here's one," I said and pulled into an open slot.

"Maybe we should call your daddy and let him

know where we are. Then he could come and drive us back to Moodus Meadows."

"But, Mama, we just got here. Come on, it will be fun. I've got money, lots of it." I picked up the straw bag and shook it so she could hear the coins inside.

"I'm not taking a step until you tell me what happened to your daddy."

"Oh, he had to work and wanted to postpone your outing until Friday, but I didn't want to wait anymore."

She smiled at me and played with one of my earrings. "You never had much patience. Okay, we'll do a little shopping."

We climbed from the car and locked it up, leaving the windows open a crack.

She took hold of my hand to slow me down as we walked toward the stores. "Someone else will have to drive us home."

"But, Mama, you said I was a good driver."

"You are, but it happens to be against the law to drive without a license, not to mention it should be against the law to wear so much makeup." She rubbed at my cheeks with a tissue.

"I was trying to look older."

Mama stared at my feet. "Are those my new shoes you're wearing?"

"They almost fit."

She laughed and hugged me to her, and I felt as if I had won the biggest prize at the carnival, the giant stuffed panda that sits on the top shelf.

"Do you think people can tell about me?" Mama asked when a woman loaded down with shopping bags smiled at her.

"You look the same as anybody else," I said. It wasn't exactly the truth. She shuffled her feet as if she didn't have the energy to pick them up and set them down again. I didn't want to force her to do anything that might set her off, so we window-shopped, peering into a jewelry-store window, pretending to be rich enough to buy anything we wanted.

"I'll buy that diamond necklace," I said.

"Too fancy. But I wouldn't mind that string of pearls. Look how they glow, Buddy. Why, they're almost pink."

"Some day when I have a job, I'll buy them for

you. And you can wear them with your blue dress when you go out with Daddy."

She squeezed my arm. "For now, I'd settle for a hamburger and some fries. I'm starving. Do you have enough money in that purse to buy your mama some lunch?"

"I've got over twenty dollars."

We decided on the Bluebird Diner, set on the edge of the parking lot, the sun bouncing off its chrome exterior. It was early for lunch, so we could have any table in the place. Mama chose a booth near the back, saying it would be quiet, so we could talk.

Compared to what she'd been through, my summer didn't amount to much, but she acted interested when I filled her in on how I spent my days at the town pool. She sat up and took notice when I let her in on how Sherry and I got Verna's daddy out of jail.

"That poor girl. I've always liked Verna. She did such a wonderful job with the costumes."

A waitress appeared wearing a pink uniform with a fancy hankie in the pocket. Mama waved away the menus and ordered a hamburger and a cup of coffee.

"I'll have a BLT with extra mayonnaise and chocolate milk, please." I smiled at the waitress and looked around the diner, which was filling up faster than a church on Easter Sunday.

Mama played with her silverware, set each piece square on her place mat, fiddled with the tines of her fork.

"So, how do you like being out and about?" I asked her. "It must be nice for a change."

Mama patted my hand and smiled. "I haven't missed shopping. And it's been nice having someone else do the cooking. Of, course, we do tidy up our rooms and take turns vacuuming and dusting the main rooms."

"But it's not as good as being in your own home. Isn't that what you always say?"

"I do miss you, Buddy, but a person can make a home almost anywhere. I think a home is wherever you feel safe."

I wanted to ask her, *What about love, doesn't that count for something?* But her eyes began to dart around as if she might be looking for a way out.

"Look, we can play some songs," I suggested as I tapped the miniature jukebox mounted on the wall next to our table. I flipped the selections and read off the titles of some of the records.

"I don't have any coins," said Mama.

"That's okay, I've got plenty. Who do you want to hear? Perry Como?"

"We don't need any music." She picked up her spoon and twirled it round and round.

"Okay. We can just talk."

The waitress returned with tall glasses of water.

I sipped mine and waited for Mama to speak. I wanted her to tell me that my breaking her out of Moodus Meadows was just what the doctor ordered, and now she knew what she was missing by staying hidden away in that place.

She smiled at me again. "So, Buddy, are you excited about going back to school?"

"Yes, ma'am. Ginger's got all kinds of ideas about what we have to do to be cool. I like her, but sometimes she drives me crazy." I regretted using the word crazy, but Mama didn't seem to notice.

"Maybe Sherry can take you shopping for some clothes. I'll tell your daddy to give her some money. New shoes too, you should get two pairs."

"I thought we could go together, same as always. If you come home next week, there will still be time."

"Buddy, I can't, not just yet."

"Why not? I need you to come home." My voice rose two octaves; people sitting at the counter turned in my direction.

"Hush, Buddy. People are staring." Mama reached across the table to cover my hand, but I sensed she wanted to cover my mouth, to keep me from saying another word.

Our food arrived; I could barely eat with my stomach doing double back flips.

"Doesn't this look good," said Mama, and as if to prove the point, she took a huge bite of her hamburger.

Ever since Booth died I'd been keeping silent about anything that might upset Mama. After biting my tongue for two years, I couldn't stand the pain one more second.

"I think you're being selfish," I said. "Daddy's gained another ten pounds since you've been gone. He works all day at the drugstore, then comes home, eats his dinner and falls asleep in his La-Z-Boy. I don't think he likes sleeping alone in your room."

Mama sipped her coffee. "Eat your sandwich, Buddy, before it gets wilted."

"Sherry's doing the cooking, which may kill us all, not that you care a simple bit."

Mama sat stone-faced. What would it take to get a reaction from her? She continued to work on her hamburger, wiping the corners of her mouth after each bite.

"Do you hear what I'm saying, Mama? Sherry is taking over the house. She's moved through the downstairs rooms like a tornado, picking up this and that, throwing out things left and right. Why, she told me she's planning on tackling Booth's room next week." I leaned in close for emphasis. "I'm tired of guarding his room from her. So if you want to save any of his stuff, you better come home."

The waitress appeared and asked if we wanted dessert. I stared at my plate, at the BLT with one bite missing. "No, thank you."

"How about you, ma'am?" she asked Mama. "Ma'am, are you all right?"

I looked up to see beads of sweat popping out on Mama's forehead and her upper lip. She clutched the edge of the table to steady her hands.

What had I done? I wished I could take back my words, but it was too late. "It's okay, Mama," I said as I slid onto the seat beside her, taking her hands and holding them, their vibration causing my own to shake. "It's okay, Mama, take deep breaths."

She breathed in and out quickly, sounding like a panting dog.

The waitress moved closer, concealing us from the other customers. "You not feeling well, sugar?"

"I think it's the heat making her sick," I said and quicker than a blink she dipped a napkin into the ice water and wrapped it around Mama's neck.

"See if that helps."

Somebody yelled that they needed ketchup, and she ran to fetch it, leaving Mama and me alone.

"Do you want to get out of here? We can go home." I stood and helped her to her feet.

"Get me to the car, will you, Buddy?" She seemed to be concentrating on her breathing.

I left the five-dollar bill Sherry had given me on the table, and took hold of Mama's arm. She leaned against me as we took baby steps past people who pretended to be busy with their lunch even though they were probably wondering what was wrong with Mama.

Shuffle, shuffle, shuffle, Mama moved with her head hung down, her arms limp at her sides, trusting me to lead the way. Every time the shakes made it impossible for her to move, I'd urge her on. "Just three more steps and we can rest," I'd say, repeating this a dozen times until we traveled across the parking lot and reached the car, its inside now hotter than a blue flame.

Mama recovered her senses long enough to realize she didn't want me for a chauffeur. "You can't drive, Buddy. Is Sherry working at JCPenney today?"

"Yes, ma'am, she's working the makeup counter."

"Go get her."

"I can't leave you in the car, it's too hot."

"Run, Buddy, get Sherry." She gave me a gentle shove.

I cranked down all the windows, settled Mama in the car, then sprinted toward the stores, pausing long enough to kick off my high heels and carry them the rest of the way.

Customers crowded the aisles of JCPenney looking for bargains. I found Sherry giving eyeshadow advice to an old lady who couldn't decide between blue or green.

"Hey, Buddy, are you shopping with Ginger?" She waved to me and said she'd be with me in a minute.

I hopped up and down trying to get her attention, to let her know we had an emergency situation.

"What's going on?" She asked after she had rung up her sale.

"I got Mama in the car and she's not feeling well and please, Sherry, you've got to do something or she's going to die of the heat out there."

Sherry yelled to the other woman working behind the counter that she'd be back in a minute, grabbed her purse and followed me outside where we found Mama lying on the backseat of the car.

"Cheese and crackers, how did this happen? You were supposed to call and cancel the outing. Where's your daddy?"

"I guess he's at the drugstore."

Sherry's mouth opened and closed, opened and closed, silent like a ventriloquist's dummy. "Please tell me you didn't drive here yourself," she said when she found her voice.

"Okay, I won't tell you."

"You are in deep shit, kiddo. Your daddy's gonna ground you for the rest of your life." Sherry sat next to Mama, taking her pulse. "Give me the keys and get in the car."

I climbed in the back with Mama, keeping to my own side. Sherry drove onto the freeway, zipping past slower cars, smoking one cigarette after another, not saying a word.

Twenty minutes later she pulled the Bel Air next to the walkway to Maple Cottage. Mama gave my arm a tug. "I'm sorry I spoiled our adventure, Buddy. Do you forgive me?" She held onto my hand, her own still shaky.

At least Mama didn't blame me for sending her off the deep end. She even managed to get out of the car and walk inside by herself.

We ran straight into our welcoming committee. Dr. Bueller stood in the entryway talking with Daddy, still dressed in his pharmacist's coat.

Dr. Bueller whisked Mama away before I had a chance to say good-bye, or to tell her I was sorry. Daddy didn't give me a chance to say boo, taking hold of my arm and ushering me outside to the small garden.

"Whatever possessed you to do such a thing? Didn't I say we'd take your mama out another time?"

"I thought if she could get away from this place for a day, she'd see it wasn't so bad out there and want to come home."

"But we were supposed to do this on Friday. The three of us. When Dr. Bueller called me at the drugstore and said he'd seen you driving away with your mama, I said, that can't be. Buddy doesn't drive, and where would she get a car?"

"I took the Bel Air. Booth taught me how to drive it."

"Apparently so. But you could have been killed, the two of you. And what if she had another spell while you were alone with her?" Daddy sat on the wall of the raised flowerbed and opened his collar.

"She did get a little nervous, but not like at the Music Hall. Nothing I couldn't handle." I wanted to defend myself, to tell him he was the one who couldn't handle Mama's problem, but then his shoulders started to tremble and I realized he was crying.

He waved me away. "Tell Sherry to take you home. I'll stay with your mama for a while."

I found Mama lying on her bed, her eyes closed. I leaned down and kissed her cheek. "This will pass," she said without opening her eyes. "You've got a kind heart, Buddy."

"I'm sorry, I shouldn't have said those things about Booth's room. I just want you home so bad."

Mama smiled. "I'm not so crazy I didn't see

through your plan. Although I almost believed you when you said you might die from Sherry's cooking."

"Are you going to tell Daddy what I said? About him gaining weight and me calling you selfish?"

"That will be our secret. Besides, how could I be angry with you? I know you tried to show me a good time because you love me."

"I do love you, and I don't want you to be sad anymore, Mama."

"Sweetie, if love could take away sadness, I'd be the happiest woman on earth. Sometimes the sadness is so deep, we have to sift through all the layers before we can find it and send it packing. That's what I'm trying to do in this place. Find my sadness."

I wanted to lie on the floor next to her bed and hold her hand until she fell asleep the way she had for me when I was little and scared about something. Sherry came and told me it was time to go. I knew she was right. It was time to let Mama get well.

CHAPTER TWENTY-THREE

I KEPT MYSELF busy at home, getting the house spick-and-span clean, taking a break now and again to go swimming with Ginger or Verna. Daddy never did ground me, but he seemed to watch me more carefully. I did whatever I could to earn back his trust.

We did take Mama out again, with Daddy driving the Buick through the countryside. We stopped at a roadside hamburger joint, and a lady on roller skates brought our food to the car, where we ate off trays hooked over the windows.

"Slow but steady wins the race," said Daddy when I asked if an outing counted if Mama never left the car. "Let her do as much as she can. She knows her limit."

For the next couple of weeks, we took Mama out for spins in the car. Dr. Bueller said she was making good progress and coming to terms with her grief over losing her only son.

The phone call I'd been waiting for all summer came while I was helping Sherry make dinner. "That was Dr. Bueller," said Daddy. "Your mama can come home the beginning of next week."

On Monday morning, Daddy took special pains with his outfit, dressing in a new pair of khaki trousers and a freshly pressed blue cotton shirt. He fretted over which tie to wear as if he were going on a first date, settling on the blue paisley one that Mama had given him for his birthday. I put on a clean white blouse and navy-blue shorts.

He dropped me off at the drugstore at nine o'clock. I wanted to go with him to pick up Mama, but he said he needed me to help Darlene. I was about to protest, when it occurred to me that maybe Daddy wanted some time alone with Mama.

"Buddy, you wait on the customers and tell anyone who needs a prescription I'll be back by noon." I smelled the Brillcreme in his hair, slicked back from his forehead.

"Don't worry about a thing. Darlene and I will do fine."

He gave me an uneasy smile. "Well, this is it. I'm going to get your mama."

"Yes, sir, this is it." I patted the door of the Buick. He drove away, slower than I expected, as if he didn't want to advertise this was the most important day of his life.

Darlene got to the store late as usual. I didn't care. It felt good to be alone behind the counter, gave me quiet time to imagine dinner that night with Mama in the kitchen. Sherry planned to make chicken and dumplings with chocolate cake for dessert. I'd wait on Mama, giving her a chance to relax and get used to being home.

According to Dr. Bueller, she was ready to move on, but he warned us we needed to be patient. He said Mama might take baby steps at first.

It helped that we got busy that morning at the

drugstore as I waited for Daddy's return. A dozen ladies from the garden club wanted ice-cream sundaes; a man needed to pick up a prescription; a bunch of kids took their time choosing sweets from the penny-candy bins. While I scooped ice cream and rang up purchases, my eyes watched the clock.

Once the hour hand passed noon, I started a countdown in my head. Now Mama and Daddy are saying their good-byes to Dr. Bueller; now they're getting into the car; they just passed Main Street on their way home; Mama's stepping inside the kitchen door, she's petting Pepper, who's going crazy slobbering all over her skirt; she's sitting on the porch sipping an iced tea with two pieces of lemon and a spoonful of sugar, Daddy by her side, his large square hand wrapped gently around her small one.

Darlene and I contended with the lunch crowd. It took all my self-control to keep from telling those people ordering grilled cheese sandwiches and ham on rye to go home and fix their own food, just so I could hang up the CLOSED sign and go see Mama. By three o'clock I began to worry. Three customers were waiting on prescriptions, and I was running out of excuses. Daddy should have been back by then.

I called home, and when I got no answer I hung up and dialed again.

"Buddy. I'm back." Daddy stepped through the rear door of the drugstore, retrieved his white pharmacist's coat from a hook and went about his business filling a prescription for Mrs. Clarke's little boy.

"So, how is she? How's Mama doing? Is she happy to be home?" I wanted a full report, right down to what she was wearing.

"In a minute, Buddy. I want to get this filled so Mrs. Clarke doesn't have to wait on it."

"What's wrong? Is Mama all right? Is she home?"

"We'll talk later, Buddy. Your mama's fine."

"I'm going home to see Mama. You've got enough help." Darlene sat at the counter, spinning herself on a stool, reading *Modern Screen* magazine.

"No, Buddy. Don't go." He put down the bottle he held and steadied it on the counter. "There's been a change in plans." He motioned for me to follow him into the nook where he kept the powders and potions locked behind glass doors.

"What is it? What do you mean, 'a change in plans'?" I tugged at his sleeve to get the answers. "Isn't Mama home?"

"Well," he said, taking a slow breath, struggling to find the words. "Your mama's left Moodus Meadows."

"I know that. You just went to get her. Dr. Bueller said she was doing real good."

Daddy sighed and leaned against the cabinet, loosening his tie. "That's true, your mama's better than she was, but she's not ready to come home. Not just yet."

"You said she left Moodus Meadows."

"Yes, I picked her up myself. We had a nice talk with the doctor and we were headed for home, got as far as the corner of our block." Daddy paused as if he were trying to remember exactly what happened. "Then your mama, she tells me, orders me, 'Stop the car.' So I did. We must have sat there for a good ten minutes with her staring at the house and me afraid to say a word."

"Was she shaking, like the night we brought her home from the Music Hall?"

"No, she appeared to be calm as low tide. She reached over and laid her hand on mine. 'Herb,' she said, 'take me to the Y.' 'What are you saying,' I asked, and she repeated herself. 'The YWCA. I think I'll stay there for a spell.'"

Even on his best days, Daddy was a soft-spoken man, so at first I thought I had misunderstood him. "It sounded like you said Mama's staying at the YWCA."

"You heard right. We got her a little room with a bath and cooking privileges. She'll be fine there for now."

My head spun with images of Mama heating up a can of beans on a camp stove in a tiny room with peeling paint, her dripping clothes hanging from a piece of rope strung across the window. I rested against the stepladder in the corner, not trusting my legs to hold me. My stomach lurched; my fingertips tingled.

"Mama's staying at the Y? That's worse than Moodus Meadows. Nobody stays there if they've got family."

"It seems your mama isn't quite ready to be with

us. She said she needs to sort things out. Whatever that means. I can't begin to understand her." Daddy's eyes filled with tears; he picked up the bottle and twisted it in his hands.

"What floor is she on?" She couldn't do this to us again. I'd help her sort things out.

"The second floor. Room two-ten." He stood behind me and placed his hands on my shoulders. "We've gotten through worse, we'll survive this. Don't go running over there trying to convince her to come home. She's got to want that for herself."

I spun round. His face crumpled; his lip quivered. "I think she's the most selfish person I've ever known," I said. "When was the last time she gave a hoot about anyone but herself? Don't we count for anything?"

He reached out to quiet me, but I ducked away from him, stumbled from the platform and ran through the store. Displays of colorful soaps and lotions blurred before my eyes. "I hate her!" I screamed. With a sweep of my arm I sent bottles of white gardenia cologne crashing to the floor.

Darlene jumped off the stool, the movie

magazine still in her hand. Shards of glass crunched under her feet as she ran to me. "You okay, Buddy?"

"I'm fine, just fine." A cloud of gardenia scent enveloped me. From the front window I could see the YWCA.

Daddy watched me from his pharmacist's perch, a pleading look in his eyes. *Don't go.* Somebody had to set Mama straight. I threw open the front door and marched over to a parking meter, shook its box so hard I thought it might spill its coins, covering the sidewalk in silver.

Maybe Mama's final act of rejection was my punishment for every mean thing I had ever done, every evil thought that had taken root in my mind.

"Stay here, Buddy!" Daddy called from the doorway. "We'll think of something."

He slumped against the doorjamb, his paisley tie hanging at half-mast, his khakis limp and wrinkled from the humidity. His sadness choked my words, and they came out in a whisper. "I have to go, Daddy."

He was still trying to persuade me to come back inside when Darlene shouted that he had a phone call. Bobbing from one foot to the next, unsure what to do, he gave in to duty and let me go.

Maybe I should have listened to him and retreated into the drugstore, with its sweet counter treats and medicines that could work miracles. But I needed to make everything come out even, to find the answer to the puzzle that was Mama. I would force her to face me, to tell me in person why she no longer loved me, why I didn't matter.

Slapping my feet against the sidewalk, I marched to the Y. Two women wearing halter tops and shorts lazed on the front stoop sunning themselves, sipping bottles of Coke through straws. A blond lady shaded her eyes with her hand to look up at me.

"Can I help you, honey? Mary and me are taking a little break, so no one's at the front desk."

I said the first thing that came into my head. "No thanks, I came to see what's on the fall schedule."

"The schedule's posted on the bulletin board next to the water fountain. If you want to sign up for anything, give a holler."

"Thanks." I gave her a little wave and ran up the last two steps and into the building. The lobby was empty; a ceiling fan whirred above me moving warm air and causing papers tacked to the bulletin board to flap like butterfly wings. The green-speckled linoleum floor spread before me, scuffed and worn.

If I'd paused to think things through I might have turned and run home, thrown myself on my bed and stayed there until someone came to get me. But anger propelled me up the stairs two at a time. Number 210 was the last room. Number 210. Mama's new home.

How could she do this to us? Didn't she act as if everything was peachy keen the last time we talked? She even asked me to send her blue dress along with Daddy so she could wear it home.

Maybe Daddy didn't have the guts to stand up to her, but I'd tell her what was what. Who did she think she was, disappointing people all the time? I'd break down the door, throw her clothes into her suitcase and drag her down the stairs by her ankles. Mama was carrying on like a spoiled brat and some-one had to put a stop to it.

I'd give her a chance to come quietly. Glancing

around to make sure I was alone, I held my breath and rapped three times on her door. When there was no answer, I tried the knob. Locked. "Mama, it's me, Buddy. Open the door."

I knocked again, softly at first and then hard enough to skin my knuckles. "Mama, please, open the door. Open the door for me, Mama."

"Are you all right, dear?" A lady carrying a mesh shopping bag filled with fruit called to me from across the hall.

"I'm waiting for the lady in room two-ten."

The fruit lady leaned close and smiled. "She's gone out. The new woman in two-ten. I saw her leave." She reached into her bag and offered me an apple. "I paint these you know. Apples, pears, bananas. I'm an artist."

"Did she say where she was going?"

"No, but she did ask what time they lock the front door, so she must have planned to be out for a while."

"Thanks," I said, and walked toward the stairs.

"Do you want me to give her a message when I see her?"

"No. I've made a mistake. I don't think I know the woman who lives in two-ten."

"I'd better get started on my new painting." She tapped her mesh bag. "Before I lose the light."

"Thanks for your help." I backed toward the stairs. "I have to get home. My mama worries if I'm late."

CHAPTER TWENTY-FOUR

I NEEDED TO get away from that place. Maybe it was fate that Mama had left her room. The good kind of fate that keeps you from doing something stupid, a crime you'll be sorry for later.

Muttering to myself, "I want to kill her," I kept my head down and stomped my feet against the pavement until I ran smack into Ginger as she left the Sweet Shop carrying a sack of candy.

"Hey, Buddy. You're just the girl I'm looking for. Wait'll you hear the news. It's just too incredible for words."

Wait'll you hear *my* news, I wanted to say. My mama's living in the YWCA across the hall from a lady who paints fruit. But I kept my mouth shut and pretended there was nothing more I wanted to hear than Ginger's incredible announcement.

"So tell me. Don't keep me in suspense."

"Okay, listen to this. My mama is on the PTA's back-to-school committee with Teresa Potter's mama Lucille, and Lucille told her that Teresa is giving a Labor Day party."

"So what?"

"What do you mean, so what?" Ginger frowned at me and gave me a gentle shove. "This is what we've been waiting for. A real high-school party. And before school even starts, which is so cool, because then we'll know all sorts of people on the first day."

She opened her bag and offered me some candy "Maybe Teresa will invite you, but she wouldn't spit on me if I was on fire, so I doubt I'll be at the top of her invitation list."

Ginger passed me a gumdrop. "That's what's so amazing. Mrs. Potter told Teresa she can't have a party unless she invites everyone in the freshman class, and her sister Maureen is going to ask some of her friends, which is great, because she's a junior and there are going to be more cute boys than you can shake a stick at."

I'd have to beat one with a stick to get him to notice me. "Well, I bet Teresa will make sure my invitation gets lost in the mail."

"No, it already came. I went by your house to see you, and I saw it in your mailbox. I got mine this morning too."

Ginger beamed as if Bert Parks had just announced her name at the Miss America Pageant. I hated to disappoint her, but she'd have to find someone else to drag to Teresa's party. I planned to spend the rest of my summer vacation trying to figure out how to convince Daddy to move before school started. How would I explain to the kids at school that Mama lived at the YWCA?

Ginger nudged me with the toe of her shoe. "Buddy, aren't you excited? I'm so glad I found you, because we have a lot of work to do between now and next Monday. If you want Jack Fletcher to notice you, he has to see you in a different light. Men love a woman with mystery."

"I'm as plain as vanilla ice cream. If you want me

to look mysterious, I'll wear sunglasses and a hat with a veil."

"I'm serious, Buddy. Jack needs to see you wearing something that's not denim or flannel."

"Like a satin gown?"

"Get serious. I mean something like one of my cute short sets." She stared at my chest. "And we'll have to do something about your boobies."

"I don't think I'll grow any by the party."

"We can get you some at Woolworth's."

"Never," I said.

Ten minutes later I found myself at the five-and-dime staring at the padded bras. Ginger held one up for me to inspect. The cups were cone-shaped, miniature spaceships.

"Let's see how it fits." She wrapped it around me to see.

"Get that thing off me." I jerked away from her and, in case anyone was watching, feigned interest in the monogrammed hankies in the next aisle.

"Are you coming or not?" Ginger wasted no time making a selection. She headed for the front of the store, a padded bra in hand.

"This is for my aunt," Ginger informed the salesgirl as she held up the bra. "If it doesn't fit, may I return it?"

"Save your receipt, hon, and tell your aunt not to wear it or we can't take it back."

Ginger paid for the bra and gave me the thumbs-up sign. I narrowed my eyes at her. I could have strangled her with that contraption.

"Okay, let's go to your house and try this on." We stood on the sidewalk outside Woolworth's. She tossed me the bag.

I let it fall to the sidewalk. "How could you do this? What if someone we know saw us buying a padded bra?"

Ginger stuck out her chest. "Well, it's obvious I don't need one, so I'd tell them what I told the salesgirl, that it's for my aunt."

"No one would believe you. Did you ever think maybe I don't want to be the laughingstock at school? Aren't I good enough to be your friend just the way I am?"

Without waiting to hear her excuses for using me as an experiment, I crossed the street against the light and didn't stop running until I got to the park.

CHAPTER TWENTY-FIVE

*A*WAY FROM the heat of the sidewalks, the park air felt ten degrees cooler than in downtown Moodus. I paused under a tree to catch my breath. My heart raced; I touched the inside of my wrist to feel the vein throb beneath my skin. Between Mama running off again and Ginger trying to turn me into her personal Barbie doll, I could spit nails.

There was no sense going home to an empty house. Even Pepper had taken off that morning to sit outside our neighbor's house and pine for their female dog, a beagle in heat.

I imagined Daddy occupied at the drugstore. In times of trial he liked to lose himself in the smallest bits of busy work. The day after Booth's funeral he had rearranged all the canned goods in the pantry and cleaned the oven.

Even Sherry, who had taken to watching over me like a guard dog, announced at breakfast she wouldn't be home for dinner.

And Mama, the woman who brought me into the world, the same person who claimed she loved me more than life itself, could be anywhere.

I perched on the steps of the bandstand and picked at the grass clippings stuck to the soles of my shoes. Mama used to bring Booth and me to the Friday evening concerts in the summertime.

Daddy joined us after work, pausing at the entrance to the park until he spied Mama waving to him, sitting on our quilt spread open, with our dinner laid out. Mama made fried chicken, hard-boiled eggs, and chocolate iced brownies, and packed them in a covered basket along with a jug of iced tea laced with mint from the garden.

We'd eat our food slowly, savoring every bite

while we listened to the music. Bits of conversations sifted through the canopy of maple leaves and rained down on us like confetti. Small children rolled around on the lawn or chased each other in games of tag.

Booth didn't need any prodding from Mama to take off with his pals. Long-legged girls in short-shorts followed them around the park and to the river's edge, where I suspect they groped each other in the dark.

"Go on, if you want to, go play with your friends," Mama would say when Ginger or some of the kids I knew from school ran past and called to me. Sometimes I went along with Ginger, but usually I stayed on the quilt and pretended to fall asleep so I could listen to Mama and Daddy whisper to each other about their day. With my eyes closed, it was easy to imagine we lived on an island in the middle of a calm and beautiful sea, our quilt a safe place for just us three. It was a private island, like one of those exclusive country clubs; Booth could not join.

Even before Booth died, there were times, more

than I like to admit, when I wished he would disappear. Not die, mind you, but simply slip away. Maybe to a fancy prep school up north, far enough from Moodus so he could come home only on holidays.

I loved him, but he was too good, too funny, too smart, too athletic. How could I ever stand out when he shined so bright no one could see me? Daddy referred to me as his quiet child, but what sense was there in speaking up when Booth was around? I was like one of those people in the background of a group photo that you have to squint your eyes to see, to make out who they are.

Some kids about my age came into the park and walked toward the river, playfully shoving each other and laughing. I slipped to the back of the bandstand and flattened myself along a bench. I hated those kids. Hated them for laughing, for enjoying their summer vacation while my own was as much fun as picking nits from my hair. Lying on the hard bench, I willed myself to calm down, listened to the whoosh of traffic from the bridge, concentrated on the fluttering sound of birds zipping from tree to tree. With the sun setting over the river, its rosy glow coloring the sky, I fell asleep, my head resting on the crook of my arm.

I awoke to the smell of smoke. A few shadowy figures gathered around one of the barbecues in the picnic area. Sparks from their fire flew into the night sky. I strode toward the group circled around the fire, my hands clenched into knots.

"Would you like a marshmallow?" asked a woman wearing a baseball cap. "We have plenty."

"No thanks," I said. "Do you know what time it is?"

"It's half-past nine," she said, and speared another marshmallow on her stick. "Sure you don't want one?"

"No thanks, I have to be somewhere."

CHAPTER TWENTY-SIX

WHERE COULD I go? It was too late to show up at Ginger's, and if I did she'd probably close the door in my face. Verna's was too far to walk.

I thought of Gram, pictured her sitting at her sewing machine, its hum soothing and familiar. She always told me, *It's a great life if you don't weaken.* I felt safe at her house, and special. I could hear her voice—*How's my girl?*

Gram sat on her porch in the big wicker rocker, facing the river. Cars moved across the bridge, their headlights streaks of white. She wore a blue-checkered housecoat and red slipper socks.

"Why, Buddy, what brings you here?" She patted the cushion of her chair. I squished myself next to her, felt her arm slip around me and pull me close. "How's my girl?"

"Not so good, Gram."

She sighed and leaned back in the rocker, taking me with her until our feet hung suspended in the air. "I heard about your mama. Your daddy called and told us. It's hard to believe my own daughter's living in the YWCA. Tess nearly had a fit. Said she was going to march over there and talk some sense into Ellen, but I told her straight out it wouldn't do her any good. Ellen is my first-born, and I love her dearly, but she is as stubborn as a swelled-up door on a hot day in August. There's no way you're going to budge her once she makes up her mind."

"She's never coming home, is she Gram?" I settled my head on her chest and listened for her heart.

She patted my head. "Don't give up on her. She'll come around, in her own time."

"Why is she so sad? I know she misses Booth, but I think there's something else. The night she went away she told me that ever since Booth and I were born she's been afraid God was going to take us away."

Gram took a deep breath; her chest rose beneath me. "I wish she wouldn't fill your head with that nonsense, but I'm not surprised. She's always been a worrier."

"It's way past worrying. She's filled with guilt." The sound of Tess's voice startled me. Gram and I flipped the rocker forward; I spied Tess behind the screened door.

"You might as well come outside if you're going to be eavesdropping on Buddy and me."

The door creaked open, and slapped shut behind Tess, who appeared with her hair wound around pink sponge rollers, her face shiny with cream. She plopped on the glider, arranging her cotton piqué robe trimmed in white eyelet around her wide hips. I had never known Aunt Tess to wear anything so fancy.

"I wasn't snooping, Mama, just getting a little fresh air. The house is holding on to the day's heat. Buddy, would you like some lemonade? I just made it."

"Not right now." Gram held tight to my hand as if she didn't want to share me with Tess.

Tess got up, walked across the porch and leaned against the railing. She sighed dramatically, a long whoosh of air escaping her thin lips.

She shook her finger in our direction. "If you ask me, I'd say Ellen blames herself if the farmers in Idaho have a bad year for beans. She's the exact opposite of Sherry. That girl wouldn't own up to snitching the cake saved for company even if you caught her with chocolate icing spread ear to ear."

I had to agree with Aunt Tess. "I think Mama believes in that original sin stuff we hear about at church."

Tess strolled back to the glider, shook off her slippers and reclined on her side. "Ellen's pretty closemouthed about her feelings, but I've got my suspicions."

Gram made a growling sound in her throat. "Keep your suspicions to yourself, missy. Don't butt in where you don't belong." Gram turned my face to hers, her bony fingers gripping my chin with a gentle touch. "How about some oatmeal-raisin cookies, honeybun?" She shifted in the rocker and I rose and helped her to her feet.

"I'll be in in a minute. I want to watch the bridge for a while. There sure is a lot of traffic tonight."

"Suit yourself. I'm going to lie down, not that I expect I'll be able to sleep. I haven't had a good night's sleep since nineteen-forty-two." She smiled at me and patted my cheek.

"Good night, Gram." I gave her a hug.

She shuffled to the door, her knees stiff. "Call your daddy so he doesn't worry where you are. Seeing how late it is, you might as well sleep over. You can have your mama's old room."

"Okay, I'll call Daddy in a minute."

I waited until Gram had time to climb the stairs to her bedroom before I sat beside Aunt Tess.

"This must be hard on you, but don't give up." She took two pieces of saltwater taffy from the pocket of her robe and passed one to me.

I untwisted the waxy paper, popped the candy in my mouth, and tasted lemon, tart and slick against my tongue. "You are so unlike Mama. It's as if you came from two different families."

She laughed and pushed the taffy to the side of her mouth so she could talk better. "All of us girls are peculiar in our own way. Look at Sherry—she's a pistol. I never know what guy she'll take up with next. And here I am, a middle-aged woman still living at home, teaching high-school phys ed, and dating a man who spends more time with his cats than he does with me. Call me weird, but I'm a contented woman. I enjoy my work, like having my independence, and get a kick out of bowling on Tuesday nights and playing bingo on Thursdays."

"I don't think you're weird."

Aunt Tess gave me a squeeze. "You're a good kid, Buddy, but I know how Sherry makes fun of me. She thinks I'm an old fuddy-duddy. But I don't take it personally."

She offered me another candy, but I was still working on the last piece. "Sherry likes to tease."

"It doesn't bother me anymore. I don't have to look in a mirror to know I'm not the prettiest flower in the garden. I don't envy Sherry her looks. Being pretty has its own problems. Now, your mama's the one who has a way of getting under my skin, making me feel like I should be doing more with my life."

"You do plenty. And what good did trying to save the world do for Mama? Look what it's done to her."

Aunt Tess fished in her pocket for more candy, but came up with empty wrappers. "I wish I could help her."

"Maybe you can. I think you might know something, a clue to why she's afraid to come home. She told me we were better off without her, as if she might hurt us. You've known her since she was a little girl, so maybe if you think real hard, you'll remember something."

The hair rollers bobbed as Aunt Tess shook her head and tucked the candy wrappers in her pocket. "I don't want to dig up the past."

"There is something, isn't there? That's why Gram changed the subject when you said you had your suspicions."

Aunt Tess stretched out her legs, and arranged a plump pillow behind her back. "I will tell you this. Your mama's grief started a long time before Booth died. I suspect she's never gotten over our brother Tommy."

I thought of the small black-and-white photo of Tommy that Mama kept in a picture frame on her dresser. No one talked much about him, except to say he got hit by a car when he was only five.

"Were you there when it happened? Was Mama there?"

"No, I didn't see it happen. I was at the dentist having a tooth pulled when someone called and told us to come quick, there'd been an accident. I still had a wad of cotton in my mouth when we got to the hospital."

"Gram doesn't like to talk about it."

"Maybe she's right, and it's not my place to say any more than I have." I started to protest, but she held up her hand to quiet me. "Talk to your mama, Buddy. Even if she doesn't want to come home, she owes you the truth."

CHAPTER TWENTY-SEVEN

I STOOD IN Gram's kitchen helping myself to a glass of milk when the phone rang. It was Daddy. "Buddy, is that you? I've been worried sick. Sherry's out looking for you."

"Sorry, Daddy. I meant to call."

"You were in such a state when you left this afternoon, I didn't know what to think. I called Ginger's house, and she told me you girls had an argument and she hadn't seen you since."

"Yeah, well, Ginger exaggerates. But I'm okay. I think I'll sleep over here tonight."

"That sounds like a good idea. Spend some time with your grandma."

"I'm sorry I upset you."

"I do care, you know that, don't you? Sometimes it may seem as if I bury myself in my work, but I think about you. I don't want to lose you, Buddy."

I could tell he was talking over a lump in his throat; I couldn't bear it if he started to cry. "You couldn't lose me if you put me on a train to Alaska. I'd find my way home."

"What was I thinking? Of course you would. Don't mind me, I guess I'm tired. It's been a long day."

I wondered if he was still wearing the paisley tie, the one he wore to impress Mama. "Good night, Daddy."

"Sweet dreams, baby girl."

I returned to the porch to sit beside Aunt Tess. We watched the river, its surface shimmering with reflected moonlight, until her eyes started to close. She came to with a start at the sound of Sherry's car pulling up to the curb. Sherry slammed the door shut and clomped up the porch steps.

"Cheese and crackers, Buddy, you had us worried. I got home from work and found your daddy looking like he ate a piece of bad fish."

"You heard about Mama living at the Y?"

Sherry squeezed between us on the glider. "Doesn't that beat the band? When Ellen decides to go crazy, she goes all out."

"Mama's not crazy. Dr. Bueller told Daddy she's doing okay."

"I didn't mean it in a bad way. I kind of admire Ellen for doing something for herself for once in her life."

We moved inside and sat around the kitchen table, finishing off the better part of a tin of cookies and a quart of ice-cold milk.

A little past eleven, Sherry left to meet Darren. Tess sent me to bed with a quick hug and a promise that everything would look better in the morning.

Mama's girlhood bedroom smelled of dried lavender. I slipped under the cool sheet, still in my clothes, waiting for the house to settle down for the night. Nestled in the maple four-poster, I listened to Gram's snores from the next room. Tess slept with the radio on, tuned to a station that played love songs. It was easy to slip a note under her door and leave the house unnoticed.

CHAPTER TWENTY-EIGHT

LET THE IRON gate to the side yard clank shut softly behind me. The street stood empty. I took a moment to collect my thoughts before I walked up the hill.

I must have paced back and forth across from the YWCA a dozen times, staring at the sidewalk, trying to get up the courage to go inside.

The front door to the building stood ajar. A young woman sat at the front desk reading a book, too absorbed to look up and see me sneak up the stairs.

Mama's door popped open before I could knock. "I saw you coming," she said. "I was sitting over there, watching you from my window." She pointed to a green wooden chair turned to face Main Street.

Alone in her room past midnight, she still wore the blue dress she had asked me to send along with Daddy when he picked her up at Moodus Meadows. I stepped over her white high heels, lying on their sides, as if she had kicked them off as soon as she walked in the door.

"I like to sit in that chair and watch people go about their business. Everyone seems in a hurry to get someplace," she said.

"You used to be like that, Mama. Doing three different things at the same time, like a juggler."

"Not anymore, Buddy. In case you didn't notice, I believe I dropped all those balls I had in the air. Now I want to stay put." Traces of lipstick edged her mouth.

Why did she go to all the trouble of dressing up if she was going to hide herself in the YWCA? I wondered if she had got herself spruced up for her homecoming and then got scared. Panicked, like that day I took her out of Moodus Meadows.

"Why can't you stay put at home? Daddy and I

will take care of everything. You can lie in the hammock all day long and we'll treat you like you're the Queen of Sheba."

"I wish I could." She fidgeted with an earring.

"It's because of Booth, isn't it? It hurts you too bad to be there with all the memories."

"I miss Booth, but it's more than that. You have to trust me, Buddy, this is best."

She reached out, but I stepped away and kicked at her shoes. One of them spun across the floor and stopped near the bed, its skinny heel pointed at me. "How can I trust you when you keep lying to me? Didn't you tell me you were feeling better, that you were ready to come home?"

"I thought I was, but when I saw your daddy standing there all dressed up, looking so hopeful, I knew I'd disappoint all of you again. I can't be the old Ellen Mullens. It just about killed me."

"So be whoever you want to be. Just do it at home."

"I can't, Buddy. Not now. I love you, but I need to live by myself. How can I make you understand this is best?"

"If I'd been the one who died instead of Booth, you'd come home. You'd do anything for him. Booth could have saved you. He could have taken away your sadness." I bit my lip to keep from crying, but the dam broke and tears ran down my face faster then I could brush them away.

Mama opened her arms to me. "Oh, sweetheart, don't say that. This is not your fault."

I stepped back, out of her reach. "But I wanted to be the one to save you. I thought if I could make you happy again, you'd love me the way you loved Booth."

"Is that what you believe, that I loved Booth more than you?"

"I wouldn't blame you if you did. The whole time you kept blaming yourself for him dying, I should have told you that it wasn't your fault. If anyone's to blame, it's me."

"Oh, Buddy, that isn't so."

"Hush up, Mama, and listen to me. I am an evil person. I used to wish he'd disappear just so I could be alone with you. I wanted to be special."

"You've always been special."

"Didn't you hear what I just said? I wanted him to disappear. But I didn't mean for him to die."

"Of course you didn't." Mama closed her eyes as if she were thinking real hard, then walked to the window and looked to the street below. "I know what it's like to want attention, to want to be special."

"But you never had a brother like Booth. I could never compete with him. He was almost perfect."

Mama turned and smiled. "To me, you were both perfect. And I do know what it's like to have a brother who's special. My brother Tommy came along when I was eight years old and he was one of those kids everyone is crazy over."

"Were you jealous of him?"

"Not so much jealous as resentful, because I was the one who usually got stuck watching him."

"Gram never talks about him."

"Yes, well, he died you know, when he was only five." I nodded at her, *Yes, I knew.* "I was with him."

"I heard Tess say it was an accident, that he got hit by a car."

Mama moved her head from side to side as if she were trying to shake away a scary picture. "Tess had to go to the dentist on account of a bad molar and I had to baby-sit Tommy. He didn't have the patience to sit quietly at the dentist's. It didn't matter that I had plans of my own to go school shopping with my friend Evelyn. Just take him along, Gram said, and promised to make it up to me later. I wish I could go back and do that day over. But we can't, can we?"

"No, Mama, what's past is past."

"But the past stays right here," she placed her hand on her heart. "And so does the truth. Our memories might fade, but the truth, what really happened, that's as clear as polished glass."

I walked across the tiny room, sat on the edge of her bed and wiggled my bottom across the chenille spread until I sat wedged in the corner against the wall. "I want to hear the truth, Mama. I want to hear the whole story."

She sat on the green chair; it creaked under her, I suspected more from the extra weight of her sorrow than from her body, as spare as a praying mantis.

"I've never told this to anyone else."

"Go ahead, you can tell me anything. You could

confess that you killed a hundred people and I wouldn't love you any less."

And so, from her place by the window, Mama opened her heart to me. She told me of that day so long ago when she was in charge of her little brother, a five-year-old boy with the energy of a tornado, who didn't like to be held on to, who pulled away any chance he got to run free and explore.

Mama moved to the edge of the bed, her face aglow as she talked about her brother. "He loved dogs, any kind of mutt, and some say that's what he was after, an old hound walking down the other side of the street."

I could picture the scene in my mind. Little Tommy pulling away from Mama, running into the street. "It could have happened when he was with Gram."

"That's exactly what she said. 'Don't you fret, sweet girl; it could have happened when he was with his daddy or me. That boy was an escape artist, a regular Houdini.'"

"So why do you still blame yourself?"

"Because that wasn't the whole story. Everyone

thought Tommy got loose from me and ran after that dog. And I let them believe they were right."

For a moment I wondered if I really wanted to find out the truth. "Tell me, Mama. I'll still love you no matter what you did."

She snuggled beside me, taking hold of my hand and letting her head drop onto my shoulder. "We passed a window, one of those big plate-glass ones, and I noticed my hair had come undone. You wouldn't know it now, but I took great pride in my looks, and I stopped to fuss at my hair, rearranging the barrettes and snapping them in place."

She sat up straight and looked down at me. "That's all it took, that one second when I dropped his little hand and he spotted that dog. I didn't even notice he was gone until I heard the screech of the car brakes. I knew before I turned, watched it all happen like a movie reflected in that window."

We held on to each other through the night. Each time I stirred, Mama stroked my brow and said, "It's going to be okay, Buddy, I'm here."

I awoke to discover Mama sitting on her chair, gazing at me. "What are you thinking?" I asked.

277

"I've been watching you all night. Just watching you sleep, the way I did when you were a baby. You're the same age now that I was when Tommy died." Tears streamed down her face, but when I made a move to get up, she put out her hand to stop me.

"Let me finish what I have to say, Buddy. Last night you said you wanted to save me, to make me better. Looking at you asleep, I realized if it had been you with Tommy, I wouldn't have blamed you, wouldn't have expected you to keep him safe all the time. You're a young girl with a kind heart, and so was I. Even then, I thought I could save the world."

I rubbed my eyes, still filled with sleep. "I don't understand."

"I look at you and I see myself at your age. I didn't want anything to happen to my little brother any more than you wanted Booth to die. Listening to you in so much pain helps me to remember what I felt at your age. It's because of you I can finally forgive myself."

"So, will you come home, now?"

"Not yet, Buddy. I've decided to take the year off, from everything. I'm going to call Mr. Peebles at the high school and ask for a leave of absence."

She said she needed to have time to herself, "time to take care of Ellen," was how she put it. I tried to understand her dilemma; Mama had been taking care of everyone else for so long, she'd misplaced herself.

I hoped what she said was true, that I reminded her of herself when she was my age. It comforted me to believe that in some small way, I'd helped her to get better.

It pained me to leave her in that room. She told me to stop wasting time and to get on with my life. "This is all we have, and we better do something with it."

CHAPTER TWENTY-NINE

I DIDN'T SO much get on with my life as have a certain bossy friend push me out there. Daddy and I sat at the kitchen table trying to look on the bright side of Mama's decision to live apart from us, when I spied Ginger cutting across our lawn.

"Tell her I went for a walk," I said to Daddy before I ran upstairs.

"Buddy, I know you're here!" she yelled up the back stairs, and a minute later she pushed open my door and came in uninvited.

"Go away, Ginger." I lay on my bed, my face buried in my pillow.

"At least try it on. If you don't like it, I'll return it to the store and say my aunt has enough bras."

Sitting up and swinging my legs to the floor, I threw my Winnie the Pooh bear at her. "I said, go away."

Ginger removed the padded bra from the bag. "You don't mean that, Buddy. Come on, aren't you curious about how you'll look with breasts? This could change your life."

"My life is already changed. For someone who claims to be a know-it-all, you're pretty dumb."

Ginger tilted her chin. "I have no idea what you're talking about."

"My mama's left us. And she might not be coming home." There, I had said it and I couldn't take it back.

"I know, Buddy."

"You don't know anything. You just think you do. Mama didn't go to Atlanta to help her friend with her babies. She's been right here all summer at Moodus Meadows."

Ginger sighed and sat next to me on the bed. "Yes, I know. I've known all along. Your mama called mine the first week she was there so she wouldn't worry about her."

"But you never said anything. You acted like you believed me when I told you she went to Atlanta."

"My mama said to wait until you said something. Until you were ready to talk about it. Why do you think I've been driving you nuts with this makeover stuff? I've been trying to take your mind off your troubles. "

"I wanted to tell you about Mama, but every time I tried, I'd chicken out. I was afraid you wouldn't want to be my friend."

"Do you really think I'm that shallow?"

"No, but I hear what you say about Verna, and there are days when I wonder if I'm okay, if I'll ever feel normal again. I wouldn't blame you if you didn't want to hang around with me."

"Buddy, we've been friends forever. I was with you when you peed in your pants in kindergarten, and didn't you lend me your sweatshirt to tie around my waist when I split my shorts at the fourth-grade picnic? Remember when we used to sleep over and stay up half the night telling each other our secrets? How could you doubt that I'd be your friend?"

"I'm sorry. I should have trusted you."

"Well, maybe you can make it up to me." A glow returned to her eyes.

"I don't know if I like the sound of this. Let me guess, I have to wear that bra."

"That's a good start. Come on, Buddy, try it on."

"Okay, but promise, if it looks awful, you'll leave me alone."

Ginger crossed her heart. "Promise."

I went into the bathroom and came back wearing the bra under my top. It felt lighter than I had thought it would.

"You look great," said Ginger. "Very natural."

I stared at myself in the mirror and poked at the two bumps jutting against my shirt. "Ginger, there is nothing natural about going from a double A to a B cup overnight. No one will believe this."

She sat on the floor and studied me. "You worry too much. Besides, all you ever wear are those baggy shirts, so no one knows what size you are."

"It will never work."

She dismissed my anxieties with a wave of her hand. "We'll do this gradually. Over the next week you'll add some stuffing to your old bras every day. Cut-up nylons look the most realistic."

I watched Ginger as she fitted my old bras with pieces of cut-up nylons I found in the bottom of Mama's sewing basket. She hummed as she worked, a truly contented person.

"By the way," I said to her as she held up my bra for inspection. "Mama got out of Moodus Meadows yesterday."

"Why, Buddy, that's wonderful. Where is she? Is she resting?"

"No, she's got herself a room at the YWCA. She's living across the hall from an artist who paints fruit. I think she wants to spend some time alone, just taking care of herself."

Ginger hugged me to her. "She'll come home, Buddy."

My eyes filled with tears and when we pulled apart, I noticed Ginger was crying too. Black smudges formed under her eyes.

She dabbed at my tears with a tissue and gave me another hug. "Remember, Buddy," Ginger said, "Never cry when you're wearing mascara."

CHAPTER THIRTY

*T*HE AFTERNOON of the party my brain short-circuited. I needed a list to get myself ready. Shower, wash hair, put on padded bra, dress in ridiculous outfit. Daddy had a Rotary Club dinner, so it was just Sherry and me puttering around the house. Ginger called every ten minutes with more instructions.

"Nervous?" Sherry asked.

I nodded my head, yes.

"You'll see, once you get to the party, you'll calm down. Besides, Ginger will be with you." Sherry sat on the bottom bunk filing her fingernails.

"Ginger's company will last until the first good-looking guy makes eye contact with her. Then I'll have to entertain myself passing out the chips and dip or dancing with Teresa's little brother."

Sherry grabbed a hairbrush and started playing with my hair. "Tonight will be different. Trust me. The boys won't be able to take their eyes off you."

We stood poised in front of the mirror, with Sherry playing beautician. She decided my usual ponytail wouldn't do, and without bothering to ask my opinion, piled it on the crown of my head, rolled it into big fat curls, and anchored them to my scalp with hairpins.

"Well, what do you think?" She turned my head this way and that.

"Sausage head," I pronounced, staring at my new look. It made me appear unbalanced.

"This is very in," said Sherry. "Just take a gander at your movie magazines. All the stars wear their hair this way to movie premieres. Grace Kelly, Joan Crawford—they know what's what." She grabbed a bottle of Aqua Net from her stash on the dresser and sprayed a cloud of it on my hair.

Choking from the fumes, I waved my hands.

"Don't touch your hair until it dries." Sherry pressed my hands to my sides.

"Don't you think this is a bit much for a luau in Teresa Potter's backyard?" I touched my hair while Sherry had her back turned. The sausage-roll curls crunched under my fingers, hard enough to qualify as protective headgear.

"You don't want to look like every other girl there, do you?" Sherry checked her watch. "Hey, you better hurry and get dressed."

I opened the door to my room. "I think I can manage that by myself."

Locking the door behind Sherry, I searched in my underwear drawer for the new padded bra. I put it on and took it off three times.

If Mama could see me she'd rip the bra from my hands and throw it in the trash. But Mama wasn't there, so I rehooked the bra and left it on. Serves Mama right, I thought, for abandoning me. Well, she did call me every night to talk, but so far she'd made no move to come home.

Sherry drove me to Ginger's. "Are you sure I look okay?" I wore the white knit top and shorts Ginger had picked out for me at Hudson's Department Store. Ginger believed in matching outfits.

"Buddy, you'll knock them dead. Teresa Potter will be green with envy." She drove around the circular driveway in front of Ginger's house and stopped the car. "Go get Ginger before you're late."

I wondered if Ginger was watching from a window as I inched up the walk, feeling as foolish as someone dressed for Halloween in April. Maybe new looks worked for Sherry and every other girl in the world, but I was Buddy Mullens. Wearing lipstick and a padded bra, I felt like a kid playing dress up. Why had I let Ginger and Sherry talk me into trying to be someone I could never be, someone cool?

"You look great." Ginger squealed when she opened the door to her house. "Doesn't she look great?" She asked her mother, Ceci, who stood in the foyer.

Ceci looked me up and down. "Fabulous. But Buddy, you could use a little color."

Ginger and Ceci looked at each other knowingly and Ginger sent her little sister Barbara Ann to the bedroom to fetch the Avon kit.

"You have beautiful eyes, Buddy." Ceci put a third coat of mascara on my lashes. If I blinked too long they would seal together tighter than a flap on an envelope. Ginger got into the act, stroking my cheeks with coral rouge.

"Perfect," they said in unison, stepping back to admire their work.

Ginger laced her arm through mine and practically skipped to the car. "I'm so excited I could pop a button. Our first high-school party, Buddy. Couldn't you just die?"

I was about to inform her I could die from embarrassment, but she had a hopeful look on her face, and I didn't want to spoil her fun.

"Va-va-voom." Sherry gave her approval as I climbed into the front seat.

"She looks gorgeous," agreed Ginger. She sat next to me, wrapping a blue silk scarf around her freshly teased and sprayed hair. "This will be so cool, showing up in your Impala, Sherry. Thanks for the ride."

"What time should I pick you up?" We sat in front of Teresa Potter's split-level house with its two-car garage. Sherry removed a small bottle from her straw bag and gave me a quick shot of her Windsong cologne.

"Enough." I reached across Ginger, jerked open the door and climbed over her, grabbing my tote bag from the floor. The padded bra shifted under my knit top. "Pick us up in an hour."

Ginger leaned into the car. "Don't listen to her. She's got first-party-of-the-year jitters. We'll call you when we're ready to come home."

"Have fun." Sherry gunned the engine and sped away.

We stood at the end of Teresa Potter's driveway. I felt as if I'd been abandoned in a strange land. I didn't belong, didn't speak the language.

"Let's go, or we'll miss something." Ginger looked at me pleadingly.

I ignored her and reached into my tote bag for a hand mirror and a pack of tissues. "This is worse than I thought. I look like Bozo the clown."

"Don't take it all off." Ginger pinched her

mouth into a scowl as I swiped at the rouge and lip-stick on my face with a wad of tissues.

"This isn't me." I looked down and didn't recognize my own chest. It reminded me of when I was seven years old and my new front teeth grew in a different shape from my baby teeth. For weeks I prayed to the tooth fairy to bring back my old teeth.

"Suit yourself." Ginger flipped her hair with her fingertips and turned away. She walked slowly along the curve of the driveway, her back rigid with anger. I had gone too far; I did not appreciate all her hard work.

I watched her check herself out in the glass panel next to the front door before she rang the bell. Someone opened the door and Ginger disappeared inside.

"Buddy, is that you?" Teresa Potter appeared around the side of the garage. She squinted her tiny eyes as she approached me, reducing them to slits. She wore blue eye shadow and had penciled her eyebrows into sharp arcs that gave her a look of surprise. "Is this real?" She touched my hair and I heard it crunch.

"No, Teresa, I'm Buddy's beautiful older sister. The one the family never talks about." I waited for her to laugh at my joke.

"Be a jerk." She waved me off like a pesky fly and strolled away.

My first impulse was to run, to get as far away from there as I could before anyone else noticed me. I would have left if it weren't for Ginger. Why had I let her talk me into coming to this party? I wished I were at Verna's playing Scrabble in her tent, with Russell in charge of the tiles.

I decided to march inside and tell Ginger I couldn't stay. I would walk home. That was the mature thing to do. I'd tell Ginger she could call Sherry when she needed a ride. That would send the message to Teresa and her crew that I couldn't care less about socializing with them.

Easier said than done. How could I face Teresa's friends in my getup? I yanked about a hundred bobby pins from my hair, and then attempted to drag a hairbrush through the tangled mess. My hair stood away from my head, stiff as starch. Hiding behind a hedgerow, I wiggled out of the padded bra.

My new white knit top looked empty, a sack of potatoes without the potatoes. I covered it with the sweatshirt I had brought along in case of emergency.

Teresa's little brother let me in the front door and led me to the patio behind the house. Dozens of kids dressed in colorful outfits stood in small groups. Red-and-yellow Japanese lanterns hung from trees; plastic lilies floated in the pool, illuminated by underwater lights. I passed a picnic table covered with bowls of chips, platters of fruit and cheese, and a bowl filled with pink punch.

I spotted Ginger talking to Brad Vickers, her obsession of the summer. She pretended not to see me, but I detected a look of disgust when she realized I had turned myself back into the old Buddy. The uncool one.

I recognized a few of the kids playing horseshoes on the lawn. Teresa stood next to a tall skinny girl, both of them dressed in tight black slacks and sherbet-colored tops. The skinny girl asked me if my coach had turned back into a pumpkin, and I realized Teresa had wasted no time telling her about my new look.

"Yeah, I left my pumpkin double-parked in the driveway, so I can't stay."

My legs seemed weighted with sand; I imagined myself moving in slow motion as I crossed the patio, trying to get to Ginger. She made a show of daintily sipping a pink drink thick with chunks of pineapple and cherries.

"Brad, you know Buddy Mullens, don't you? My best friend?" She said this with a sarcastic tone.

"Hi, Brad. Nice shirt." He wore a Hawaiian-print top and white slacks. Very tropical. "I'm not staying, Ginger. Call Sherry at home and she'll pick you up."

Brad played with Ginger's hair, winding a long strand around his finger. "I'll give her a ride home."

"Are you sure?" Ginger gave me the evil eye before I could make things worse and tell her I didn't think her mama would like her going home with a boy.

"Yes, Buddy, I'm sure."

"Okay, then. Have fun," I said as I backed away.

Ginger rolled her eyes. "I can't believe you're doing this."

I glanced over at Teresa. She played with the miniature umbrella in her drink and stared at me.

"I'm sorry," I whispered to Ginger.

She shook her head. "Forget it. Besides, he's not even here."

"What do you mean?"

"Jack. I heard Teresa whining that he isn't coming. Some excuse about his grandparents' anniversary party."

My heart took an extra beat. I reached out and squeezed Ginger's hand. "Thanks for telling me."

I smiled at Teresa as I strode past her. The smirk vanished from her face. Let her wonder where I was going.

CHAPTER THIRTY-ONE

*A*FTER MY great exit, I stood in the road, unsure what to do next. It was too early to go home. Sherry would want to know why I had left the party so early.

To kill time, I took a detour and walked down Spring Street toward the river. The street ended in a circle surrounded by pine trees.

I climbed down the bank and eased through the bushes. A branch covered with prickers snagged my knit shorts and scratched my bare leg. I was so busy trying to blot the drop of blood oozing from my skin, I almost didn't see Jack Fletcher perched on a rock, a fishing pole in his hand, the line pulled out with the tide. I tried to leave before he saw me.

"Hey. Don't run away." He laughed and recast his line.

"I'm not running away. I thought I dropped something."

"Would you like a bottle of pop?"

So this was why he hadn't shown up at the party. "No thanks. I had some punch at Teresa's."

His shrugged his shoulders and reeled in his line. "I meant to go, but . . ."

Now it was my turn to smile. "I know, you had to go to your grandparents' anniversary party. Are they hiding behind that tree?"

"Pretty lame excuse, huh? Teresa and her friends are okay, I just hate parties."

His faded T-shirt had a small hole on the shoulder. Streaks of dirt covered his shorts and his toes poked through the ends of his tennis shoes. I loved everything about him. Even his voice sounded lovely, the cadence of his words as measured as poetry.

"I do, too," I said quickly. "Hate parties. I only went because I promised Ginger, but then Brad

Vickers showed up so she didn't need me anymore. I don't really hang around with Teresa and her friends." There, I had admitted it; I wasn't one of them. As if he couldn't tell from looking at me that I was not cool.

He began to pack up his bobbins and bait. "Yeah, I know how that is, getting dragged to a party. I just wasn't in the mood tonight. I felt like coming here."

"This is sort of my place." What a stupid thing to say. "What I mean is, my brother Booth and I used to come here. We'd tell our mama we were going to Murphy's Beach over by the boat club, but we'd come here instead. The water's deeper and it's quiet. Not a lot of little kids."

Jack leaned back on his elbows and gazed at the water. "This time of day it's real peaceful. I thought I was the only one who knew about this spot. It's kind of hidden. I found it one day when I was hiking."

I wanted to study his face, to memorize the angle of his cheekbone, the curve of his lips, the golden tips of his dark eyelashes. Instead, I looked out over the water and to the rooftops of the houses on the other side.

"Have you lived here all your life, Buddy?"

I liked hearing him say my name. "We've always lived in Moodus. Every relative as far back as I can count has lived and died right here." I sat down on the grass and retied my shoe. "Except for my brother Booth, he died away at school. In a car wreck. But it wasn't his fault, he was a good driver."

Maybe it was being back at the river that caused me to talk about Booth. I hadn't been to our place since he died. Saying his name seemed only right. If Mama could keep his room intact, why shouldn't I talk about him? How else would anyone know he had lived, that he mattered?

Jack sat up and leaned toward me, the setting sun pink on his face. "So that's your brother, the guy on the plaque in the front hall of the high school?"

"Yes, that's Booth. I picked out the picture. The principal wanted to use his yearbook photo, but he looked too serious. I gave him one of Booth standing at the top of the Empire State building. His blue eyes matched the sky."

"He sure won a lot of awards. All those letters in sports and the National Merit Scholarship."

"They left out the best thing. The best thing about Booth."

"What was that?" Jack moved closer. I noticed a scar in the shape of a crescent moon over his cheekbone and imagined him as a little boy, falling off his tricycle, hitting the pavement hard.

"Booth didn't have a mean bone in his body."

"He'd put me to shame."

"Me too." It was true what I said about Booth. He could forgive anyone anything. Maybe even me for wanting him to disappear so I could be Mama's favorite.

"You're not like those other girls; you couldn't be mean if you tried." He gazed up at the sky. "It's getting dark."

The party would be in full swing by now, the Japanese lanterns casting a warm glow over the patio. Teresa would change the records from fast dances to slow romantic songs. I imagined Ginger and Brad hanging on to each other, swaying to a sad tune, one about losing the only love of your life.

Jack touched my arm. "I don't think it's a good idea for you to stay here by yourself."

"You're right. It's getting kind of cold."

He followed me up the bank carrying his bag and fishing pole. "Okay if I walk with you?"

"Sure, but don't you live in the opposite direction?" What a stupid thing to say. Now he'd know I had asked about him, found out where he lived.

"I'm not in any hurry." He smiled and walked alongside me. "So, can I walk you home?"

For once I wished Ginger or Sherry could whisper in my ear what to say. "Sure."

Strolling past the shops on Main Street, we passed the YWCA, and I glanced up at Mama's darkened window, the shade pulled down halfway. I imagined her awake in her narrow bed, listening to sad songs on the radio, watching shadows play on her walls.

"We turn here," I said. The blue lights from televisions flickered in living rooms; sounds of laughter seeped through the screens of opened windows.

"This is my street," I said, pointing to the sign on the corner. "Thanks for walking me home."

"You're welcome. But we're not there yet." I looked down at the pavement, afraid to let him see my eyes. Daddy once told me everything I felt was right there in my eyes for anyone to see.

"You okay, Buddy?"

I looked up. He smiled at me, a slow, easy smile that made me dizzy with love. "Yeah, I'm okay." I wished I lived far away, so we'd need to walk all night.

"That's my house," I said. The porch light made it look warm and inviting. We sat on the steps, me on the top one, Jack just below me, searching the sky for stars.

"Look, Buddy," he said, pointing to the night sky. "It's the Big Dipper."

"Yeah, the Big Dipper. It's still there."

He turned to face me.

Suddenly, a ruckus exploded behind me. Pepper scratched at the frame of the screen door, whining to beat the band.

"I better go in." I stood slowly, reluctant for the evening to end. "Hush up, Pepper."

Jack backed down the walk. "See you at school."

"See you there." Say something wonderful, something funny, I told myself, but couldn't think of anything better than "Thanks again for walking me home."

I slipped inside the house, closed the wooden door and collapsed against it, holding my breath.

"Hey, Buddy. Was that him? Was that Jack?" Sherry sat on the sofa in the darkened living room, next to Darren, who'd fallen asleep sitting up.

"Were you spying on us?"

"I took a peek out the window and when I saw you had company, I sat here like a quiet little mouse."

Sherry turned on the light next to the couch. Darren sat up straight and rubbed at his eyes. "Oh, hi, Buddy. I guess I fell asleep."

Sherry motioned me to follow her into the kitchen. She opened two Cokes and passed one to me. "He's a mighty cute boy."

"And he's nice, Sherry. He's better than nice, he's sweet and interesting and not a bit stuck on himself." It was lucky she was there to talk to or I might have burst with all the words I had inside me.

Sherry didn't seem disappointed that I had ditched the party. We called Teresa's to make sure Ginger had a ride home and that it was okay with her mama. Then we settled at the kitchen table with our drinks and a bag of barbecue potato chips to talk about boys and decide what I should wear on my first day of high school.

It wasn't until the end of that long day when I was tucked in bed, about to fall asleep, that I realized I had spent the whole evening without worrying over Mama. Oh, I had thought of her when we walked past the YWCA, but my guilt and anger lay quiet. It just felt right to be out having a good time. Didn't Dr. Bueller tell us we had to get on with our lives? He said it was okay to treasure our memories, but we couldn't linger in the past or we'd have no future.

Booth was dead; no amount of grieving could change that. But in the short time I knew him, he taught me a lot. *Keep quiet when you've got nothing to say, hug anything that will let you, and no matter what you're doing, have a good time.* He'd want us to take the Bel Air for a spin, lower its ragtop and let the wind whip our hair across our eyes. We'd sing along to the radio, shouting *la-la-la* when we forgot the words, and we'd point to the night sky at the first sight of the Big Dipper.

Mama wasn't to blame for losing her way; grief gets a tougher hold on some people than others. But there's nothing to be ashamed of if you put your sorrow on the back burner for a while and are good to yourself.

CHAPTER THIRTY-TWO

*S*HERRY AND I spent the rest of the week-
end clearing out Booth's room. She decided she
liked living with Daddy and me, away from Tess's
busybody ways. For once, she was in charge of running the show.

"It's time you have your room back to yourself,"
she said. I agreed, because it was what she wanted.
I'd miss our middle-of-the-night talks.

Sherry did most of the work, sorting through
Booth's things, while I sat on his bed, and decided
what we could not part with. I set aside a few of his
sweaters for Verna's brother, Russell, and kept his
quilt for myself.

After everything was boxed up and labeled we did some belated spring cleaning. I dusted and polished his dresser, taking care to make its honey-colored wood gleam like new. When I finished, I set out two framed photos, one of Booth and me sitting in the Bel Air, taken on the day he left for college. The other picture was of Mama, looking no more than thirteen, wearing a Sunday dress, with her little brother, Tommy, his hair slicked back from his smiling face, perched on her knee.

The night before the first day of school, Sherry slept above me one last time. There was so much to think about; so much had happened in that short space of summer.

In those last days of eighth grade, before Mama left, I'd daydreamed of long days spent reading thick books, lazing in the grass next to our pond and cool nights camped out with Ginger or Verna in my tent. I knew Mama was sad, but I never imagined she'd leave. I'd counted on her being close enough to hear me if I called to her.

Sherry and I talked about our summer late into the night, trying to make sense of everything.

When I couldn't fall asleep, Sherry told me to count my blessings.

We took turns, listing anything good that ever happened to us. Sherry mentioned Darren about a million times. I said I was grateful Mama was out of Moodus Meadows, and felt lucky to have friends like Ginger and Verna. I included Jack in my list of friends, but hoped for more. Just before I drifted off to sleep, I thought of another blessing.

"Hey, Sherry."

"What is it?"

"I wanted you to know the best thing that happened to me this summer."

"Let me guess. It has something to do with that boy you're sweet on."

"No. Take another guess."

"I'm too tired. Tell me, Buddy, what's the best thing?" she asked, her voice already thick with sleep.

"You came to stay."

CHAPTER THIRTY-THREE

GINGER'S MAMA dropped her off at seven so we could walk to school together like always. She ate toast with grape jelly while Sherry finished ironing my blouse.

I was standing on the porch saying good-bye to Pepper when the phone rang. "It's your mama," said Sherry.

My hand shook as I took the phone from her. Ginger signaled she'd wait outside, giving me some privacy.

"I didn't want you to leave for your first day of school without telling you good luck." Mama's voice sounded strong and sure.

"Thanks, Mama. Maybe I'll come by after school. Not right away, because I'll probably do something with Verna or Ginger. But maybe later, if I have time."

"I almost came by this morning, to make you a good breakfast, to see you off." There was such a long silence. "But I couldn't, Buddy. You understand."

"Yes, Mama, I do, and it's okay, because Sherry made silver-dollar pancakes, and she even packed me a lunch. A bologna sandwich, potato chips, and an apple. Starting tomorrow I'm on my own because, well, I'm old enough to do for myself."

"I always said you were born old, Buddy. But if it's all right with you, I'd like to make you dinner one night."

"That's sounds good." Sherry gave me a nudge and pointed to the kitchen clock. "Sorry, Mama, but I've got to go or I'll be late for school."

"You run along. And Buddy . . ."

"Yes?"

"I'm moving out of the Y today. And I wanted you to know where to find me."

"Where are you going?" I looked over at Daddy, who smiled as if he were in on her secret.

"Oh, I thought I'd try living in that little apartment above the drugstore. Since I'm taking a year off from the high school, I'm going to help out your daddy with the customers, the way I did when we were first married. By the way, that apartment needs some decorating. I'll bet you and Verna could stitch up some curtains."

"Yes, we will. I'll bring over some of those articles you're always cutting out of *Woman's Day* and get paint samples at the hardware store."

I reached over to daddy and squeezed his hand. It had been the longest, weirdest summer of my life. Maybe I hadn't convinced Mama to come home, but she was moving closer.

Sherry wouldn't let me leave until she applied a coat of Persian Melon lipstick to my mouth and dabbed a few dots of color on my cheeks.

"Buddy Mullens, don't you trip over all those boys who are going to fall at your feet," she said as she slipped a five-dollar bill into my book bag. "That's for after school, for Cokes and fries."

She glanced at the clock, yelled, "I'm late again for work," and ran out to her car. I watched as she drove away, her silver bracelets bouncing against her wrist as she stuck out her hand and waved.

Daddy and I stood alone in the kitchen. "I can throw on my clothes and give you a ride to school," he said.

"Thanks anyway, but we want to walk."

He smiled at me. "I understand. I guess it's not cool to get a ride from your daddy."

Sometimes I wished I could see myself through his eyes. "Daddy, I'm not cool now, and I never will be cool. Booth was cool; I'm just Buddy." I gave him a hug and whispered in his ear. "But that's good enough for me."

Verna stood on the corner near the elementary school where she had dropped off Russell and Tammy. A teacher had arranged for some ladies to take turns caring for her mama, Rina, and her baby sister, Jane, so Verna wouldn't have to miss school. Verna fairly sparkled, her hair brushed shiny and held in place with a black-velvet headband. She wore my blue shirt, still brand new. I had told her it didn't fit me right. Her gray cotton skirt with the kick pleat in back came from Ginger. She'd explained to Verna she'd be doing her a favor to take it because her mama wouldn't buy her new clothes until she cleaned out her closet.

"How are you doing, Verna?" Ginger turned up the collar on Verna's shirt, and then posed next to her, pulling me into the group and arranging us as if a photographer were going to snap our picture. "Well, now, I think we are going to be the best-looking freshmen at Moodus High."

Verna crossed her eyes and wiggled her nose. "I'll be happy if they let us in. I heard the sophomores stand at the front door to the school and give the freshmen a hard time. You know, tease them and ask for their passports."

"That's why we have to stick together," I said, and we latched arms, moving along the sidewalk like a triple-wide trailer, daring anyone to break us apart.

We marched along Main Street, past the firehouse, the library, and the drugstore, still locked up from the night before. Soon Daddy would arrive, slip into his crisp white jacket, and turn the sign hanging in the front window from CLOSED to OPEN. It was comforting to know I could always find him there among his pills and potions, doling out a kind of magic.

As we neared the YWCA, I told myself to keep looking straight ahead. Keep going, Buddy, I urged, but a flicker in my heart caused me to look up, and I caught sight of Mama sitting on her green chair by the window.

It's true, she didn't live with us, didn't wake me in the morning, or check on me in the middle of the night, but for her, living apart from us was a kind of medicine, what she needed to get well.

Standing there on that beautiful September morning, my first day of high school, I remembered back to when I was five years old. Sitting in the front row of the Music Hall, attending my first magic show, I watched in awe as the magician waved his wand and made a tiny French poodle sitting inside a red lacquered box disappear. *Poof!* In an instant, the dog was gone. When I started to cry,

Mama told me the poodle didn't really disappear. She said, just because you can't see something, can't touch it, it doesn't mean it isn't still there somewhere.

Booth's death had left a hole in my heart that nothing would ever fill, but it taught me that once we love someone, they are never far away. Booth is everywhere. He is in the river where we swam; he is in the quilt that kept him warm; he is in the stars, his spirit alive in the Big Dipper that shines ablaze in the night sky.

When Mama's spirit went away, it seemed as if a magician had waved his wand and made the real Mama disappear. I tried so hard to make her whole again, to find her and bring her home. Just when I thought I'd lost her forever, I realized she was like the little dog hiding behind the curtain; she had never really left us, not in her heart, where it counts. No matter where Mama lived, at the YWCA, or in the apartment above the drugstore, she would remain close to me.

"Go ahead, I'll catch up to you," I said to Ginger and Verna.

Walking toward the Y, I waved my arms in Mama's direction. Our eyes met and I blew her a kiss. She caught it and blew one back to me. I reached out for her kiss and placed it on my cheek.

"Come on, Buddy," shouted Verna and Ginger from where they waited on the corner. "We're going to be late. Hustle your bustle."

Even as I turned away from Mama, I felt her presence, a gentle hand pressed to my back, urging me forward, the way she had so long ago, on my first day of school. Maybe Mama's change of heart, her need to live alone, was her gift to me. The key to my own freedom.

"Hey, Buddy," said Verna when I caught up to her. "The way you're dragging your feet, I thought we lost you."

I linked arms with both of my best friends. "I got lost for a little while, but I'm back. I'm back for good."